LIKE WATER
AND OTHER STORIES

Like Water

AND OTHER STORIES

Olga Zilberbourg

This is a work of fiction. Names, characters, places, and incidents are either the product
of the author's imagination or are used fictitiously.

Publications by WTAW Press—a not-for-profit literary press—are made possible
by the assistance received from individual donors.

Designed by adam b. bohannon

Publisher's Cataloging-in-Publication data

Names: Zilberbourg, Olga, author. | Pursell, Peg Alford, editor.
Title: Like water and other stories / Olga Zilberbourg ; edited by Peg Alford Pursell.
Description: Santa Rosa, CA: WTAW Press, 2019.
Identifiers: LCCN: 2019901322 | ISBN 978-0-9988014-9-0 (pbk.) | 978-1-7329820-0-0 (ebook)
Subjects: LCSH Russian Americans--Fiction. | Emigration and immigration--Fiction. |
Motherhood--Fiction. | Short stories, American. | BISAC FICTION / Short Stories (single
author)
Classification: LCC PS3626.I4859 L55 2019 | DDC 813.6--dc23

Manufactured in the United States of America and printed on acid-free paper.

To my family

CONTENTS

ARTIST STATEMENT

Olga Zilberbourg was born in 1979 in Leningrad, USSR, came of age in St. Petersburg, Russia, and in 1996 moved to the United States. In 2006, she began publishing her fiction simultaneously in Russian and in English. To date, three books of her short stories have appeared in Russia; this is her first collection to come out in the United States.

Zilberbourg composed the stories in this book in the course of three years, beginning shortly after the birth of her first child. These fictions do not present the writer's experience in a literal or chronological way. They invite the reader to consider the way becoming a parent turns one's lived experience into a battleground for potential identities. The lines between the past, present, and future become blurred in the anxieties of moment-to-moment child care. Placing the brief, one-line or one-paragraph character sketches and thought pieces next to the more conventional short stories, Oz's writing highlights the process of becoming. Typically, we think of published stories as "finished"—but, as most writers know, a "finished" story is a kind of fiction. In the process of maintaining a dual, bicultural identity, the artist never fully adapts, never fully belongs, never stops becoming. She keeps growing—alongside her children.

LIKE WATER
AND OTHER STORIES

Rubicon

The spring came on hard and much too early this year, which must be why the dimensions of reality shifted. It was a January afternoon in San Francisco. The sun was shining. I was on my way to pick up my son from preschool, about to cross the street and enter a small undernourished park before climbing the final hill to the school.

A shiny red Jeep veered out of traffic. It made a left turn and pulled onto the crosswalk in front of me. The word "Rubicon" in blocky silver letters shone on its side. Behind the wheel was this kid I used to be close to in Russia, back in the 1990s, still seventeen on this day in 2018, the shock of chestnut hair cresting high over his forehead. On the sleeve of his overcoat snow was quickly melting. He leaned down and through the open window handed me a TDK compact cassette, the exact kind he and I used to exchange in high school.

He had no time to spare for "Hello, long time no see," "Hey, check out my ride," or "Where the hell are we?" Nothing like that. Not even a smile—his face remained completely blank. It was as though we were still in high school and he was terrified that his buddies would spot us. What! He was talking to a girl in the bright light of day! And not any girl, but this girl, who had her head either in the books or in the clouds. Next thing you know, he'd be carrying her backpack and buying her ice cream. The serious-looking girls were the quickest to turn men into lap dogs.

I, too, stayed mute throughout this transaction. The sudden shift in spacetime had left me speechless; but then I'd always become tongue-tied when this boy approached me. At forty, I was no wiser than at seventeen. I didn't even have enough presence of mind to scold him for reckless driving and blocking the crosswalk in his massive car.

He didn't stick around to wait till I gathered my wits. With the slightest nod in my direction, he pushed the gas pedal and took off, leaving me in a fog of fumes in the middle of the sidewalk.

Staggering, I made it to the park, the cassette tape still in hand. The sun blazed, but when I looked up, the sky seemed blindingly dark. Born-and-bred Californians never forget their sunglasses, but I walked out into the sunlight unarmed. Without protection, I could hardly see anything other than the outlines of things. But I smelled the grass, drying in the sunshine before it had a chance to grow, the purple leaf plum trees, blooming weeks before their time, and past them, the invasive eucalyptus trees, shedding their bark. Everything wanted water.

As I walked toward the preschool, I knew that my son was no longer a four-year-old with curly hair and paint on his face, but a man, a teacher, and he was waiting so he could help guide me home.

When I was a little girl and shared a single room with my engineer parents and an older brother, I'd overheard them discussing a scientific theory that the past, future, and present exist simultaneously in different parts of spacetime. I remember, lying on my green couch, trying to fall asleep, and instead picturing myself as an old woman, living, unrecognized, next door. Terrified, I slid into my parents' bed for comfort. In the years since, I'd spent a lot of time pondering this theory, trying to work out the paradoxes of quantum physics in everyday reality. I'd never expected it to all come crashing down on me one unreasonably warm and redolent January afternoon. My body was shaking with emotion and my breathing became labored as I nearly ran to the top of the hill, eager to see my son.

He was waiting for me in the classroom, and he was still four years old, but as he took me by the hand and led me back outside, he asked, "How was your day, Mommy?" He could've been thirty. "I'm hungry," he said. "We had fish for lunch. I didn't like it. I threw it away."

We found our way home. I gave him his dinner and bath, waited till he tired himself out jumping over pillows and running in circles, pretending to be an airplane, guided him into the bed and patted him to sleep. My husband came home late from a conference, laid out his haul of pens and tote bags on our kitchen table, and disappeared into the bedroom. He came back to the door when he noticed that I wasn't following.

"What's up?" he asked.

"I just need a few minutes."

The house quiet, I rummaged through our hallway closet, where after some time, I dug out my ancient Walkman. It had no batteries, but we kept a stack of spares for our son's talking books and radio-controlled cars. I dropped the tape in and, needing a break from the accoutrements of everyday life, walked outside.

The evening temperature had barely cooled, and the air felt stifling. Not far from our front door, the gingko tree was shedding golden leaves. I tried to convince myself that nothing unusual was happening. This was San Francisco, after all, and things were always blooming and shedding, without any particular pattern that I could discern. I'd lived here for years but in many ways was still a stranger.

I fingered the "play" button, gathering the stamina to press it. There had been other tapes before this one. He'd introduced me to The Doors and Nirvana, and I had recorded selections from the early Beatles for him. I'd shied away from being too obvious, from songs I really wanted to give him, like "Love Me Do" and "Eight Days a Week," and went with more whimsical ones, like "Baby's in Black" and "Norwegian Wood." The last mix I received from him was of a Swedish band, Army of Lovers. After a few melodic songs, there was a track that confused me at first, but then, putting a few things together, I was able to understand it as recorded imitations of the sex act performed by a chorus of participants. I'd hyperventilated, listening. If mix tapes were our main means of communication with one another, this one meant, what? Don't be such a prude, give a little? He was telling me to relax and have fun. Of course, he was also testing me, whether I'd be upset or not. I took it as a confirmation that he wanted too much, too fast, and I cried a lot, but at the end found no answer to give him.

So, what could be worse than sex on a mix tape? I pressed the "on" button. It rolled without making any sound except the quiet mechanical whirr. As it went on long enough, I decided that I didn't care what was on the tape. I just wanted there to be something, anything.

Listening to the white noise, I recalled what I knew about this guy's adult life. At the time of the mix tapes, he'd thought of becoming a doctor, and, after we graduated, went into a medical program. I went to the United States for a degree in computer science, and by the time I returned to Russia to visit my parents, things had taken a different turn. He'd gotten caught up in the chase for easy money, running financial pyramid schemes and unsavory real estate deals, and had been preoccupied with knowing what make of car I drove in America. Some years later, he came to pick me up for dinner in a car with a driver who was also his bodyguard. I asked him why he needed a bodyguard, and he beamed: "That's what success looks like, baby!" He took me to a hair-raisingly expensive rooftop restaurant and, seated across the table from me, kept glancing left and right over his shoulders. The food, when it arrived, came out on gold-encrusted plates. He clicked the rim with his nail and turned to me a delighted face. "They don't have restaurants like this in the US, do they?" I asked about his day job, but his answers were vague; instead he gushed about parachute jumping and snowboarding. That was the last time I saw him. During subsequent visits home, I preferred to stay off his radar.

The music started suddenly, with barely a transition, and it wasn't what I'd expected. The notes were rich and swaying, and right away I knew what it was and anticipated the words. Louis Armstrong, "What a Wonderful World." There was no holding back the tears then—I sobbed so hard, I could barely hear the music.

I'd been standing a few steps outside my house, leaning against a tree and, to stop the tears, I started looking around, hoping to achieve that state of heightened awareness the lyrics called for. But what I saw in front of me were the ruins of my house, the entire street crushed to the foundations by some nameless earthquake of the future. I closed my eyes and took a deep breath. I tried to tell myself that this was nothing but a common anxiety, the one I'd had ever since moving to San Francisco. The disasters of the future—yes, they existed somewhere on the continuum. One needed a heart of steel to bear this fact of the continuum, of which the cassette in my Walkman was the undeniable proof.

I waited to see what was to come after the Louis Armstrong tune, but the rest of the tape was empty. I fast-forwarded in short bursts. There was nothing else on the front side, and nothing on the back. The eerily earnest lyric about babies who cried as they grew was to be the only message I got. I guess I should've been glad that the seventeen-year-old I used to know found the world wonderful and wanted to share his joy with me. But I couldn't help but mourn the person he became in his adulthood. He and people like him didn't seem to care how much sorrow and destruction fast money created around them. So, he liked to pretend that we lived in a wonderful world while he drove around in his gas-guzzling car and ate nearly extinct fish from a golden plate? I took this tape as his unconscious admission of culpability.

At home, everything was quiet. The hallway still smelled like the hundred-year-old lady who'd lived here at the end of the 20th century. I checked on my son, who was still four, and asleep, grasping a miniature fire truck in his hand. In the bedroom, I undressed and lay down next to my husband. Somewhere out there, that kid was still a kid, procrastinating on his homework by making me a mix tape. Somewhere out there, I was still seventeen, lying on my stiff little green couch by the light of the moon, afraid to go to sleep for the fear that there would be no tomorrow, that I would cease to be, and that I and everyone I loved had already turned to dust.

Her Left Side

Teaching herself to fall asleep on her left side in the early weeks of pregnancy, she spent what seemed like days in bed, with her eyes closed, planning breakfast. She was torn between a porridge of roasted buckwheat groats that she bought at the Russian store, topped with milk and slices of boiled beef frank, and an American-style omelet with bacon, cheese, and ham. What would bring her more comfort? For the baby's sake she needed vegetables in her diet. Vegetables.

As a child, with a couch for a bed, she had been taught to sleep on her right side. Her grandparents, all three of them *serdechniki*, sufferers of heart disease, taught her to avoid the left side, to avoid putting weight on her heart. She now lay on her left side, as recommended by the American Pregnancy Association, and worried about breakfast. She pictured adding a single slice of tomato to her sandwich. A mistake. Bile seeped into her mouth. The baby would be a boy, she was sure, a dark-haired child after her grandfather. In bad temper, he would throw dishes across the room and blame her for the ills of the world.

A Wish

The child, whose birthday it was, spent most of the party in her room, standing in front of a daybed, head resting on the pillow. When the time came to cut the cake, several adults, in turn, asked her to go to the living room. The answer was, No, she didn't want to. No, she didn't want to blow out the candles, the four trick candles that relit after she blew them out so that every child at her party could have a go. No, she didn't want to make wishes that could not come true because the candles wouldn't go out. No, she didn't want to have the Happy Birthday song sung to her, the way it was always sung for birthdays, happy or not. No, she didn't want to smile and feel special like everyone who had that song sung to them was supposed to do. No, she didn't want to have her picture taken, especially if it meant that the trick candles would have to be relit. No, she didn't want to help her mother slice the cake, decorated with a wise owl that would have to be cut into pieces. No, she didn't want to eat the cake that would leave her feeling thirsty and then wanting more cake, though she was only allowed one slice. No, she didn't want any of this, and worst of all was the knowledge that she would have to go through this routine, because it happened to be her birthday and the kids and the adults were there to witness how she would do.

Her mother came and prodded her to the living room.

Was it really that bad? she was asked after the song was over.

Yes, she answered seriously, unable to look away from her mother's hand that was slicing through the owl's body.

Yes, she thought later, after the cake was cut and the pictures taken, and she was back in her room, standing by the daybed, thinking her thoughts.

She collected her favorite things—a hairless doll, a notebook with stickers gifted to her on a previous birthday, a broken watch that showed stopped time—on her pillow and she hugged that pillow and made a wish that she was certain would come true because it was secret and nobody could trick her out of it.

Evasion

The growth spurts came every few years and pushed our bodies exponentially upward and out. As children we moved from our cozily canopied cribs to well-padded toddler beds to twins to futons and plain mattresses on the floor (unless our families were wealthy enough to provide the modular ever-expanding bed frames) and then, as we grew on and on, we continued to move houses. Condos in the city were advertised "Perfect for thirty-somethings with children."

The forty-year-olds required higher ceilings, taller furniture. An occasional forty-year-old, nostalgic for her childhood, tried dating a twenty-something, but the romance was physically difficult to sustain. She had to crouch down to him, and he could not, on his own, open the door to her fridge and take out the pot of beans. There were, of course, young people who prided themselves on their early maturity.

The fifty-year-olds moved out to the farms, where they could shrug off the sense of being forever cramped, straighten their shoulders, and occupy themselves with tending to corn and sunflowers, apples and walnuts. At eighty, their parents grew so large and inert that talking to them was like trying to reach the top of a mountain. The eighty-year-olds were no longer heard, not even by their peers. Each of them was a heap of solitude, better able to commune with the clouds than with their fellow humans. Tending to these elderly was a challenge, for even the discovery of all the nooks and crannies where they hurt required of the younger generations long and arduous journeys. The sixty-year-olds were best suited for this work. The sixty-year-olds were still agile enough to really get in there, and the abounding apprehension of their own growth to come gentled their touch.

Seventy-seven, one woman decided, was a good age to die. She could still see her grandchildren, and she was heard when she asked her son to bring them closer, though already she was afraid to pick them up for the fear of accidentally crushing them. An apple tree could hear an oak, but to an oak the words of a giant sequoia sounded like rustling. This woman scribbled a note in the smallest handwriting she could muster, "Enough." Then she took sleeping pills and wrapped her head in plastic.

Graduate School

The English department had a stench to it. It was the morning after spring break, and Sonya had put off grading the essays far too long. She sat down in the faculty reading room, where people could see her at work, and pulled out a green pen. Her comments would be generous, insightful, plainly phrased. But the essays were awful. One eighteen-year-old argued that people who didn't believe in God were inviting misery and suffering into their lives. Another, a young man, wrote, "Thus, school uniforms are necessary to protect women from dressing however they want for their own good." Sonya lifted her head. The reading room was empty.

That afternoon a biohazard truck obstructed the exit from the Humanities building. Sonya went home to drink wine and read her email. She'd been collecting rejection letters from the PhD programs she'd applied to; waiting in her inbox was the last of the bunch. A PhD in literature was likely to land her, six years later, in the same job, grading the same essays. The only difference would be that a PhD made her eligible for a tenure-track position. She would never see the end to grading. Perhaps these rejections were a blessing in disguise: it was time to move on from teaching. Once, she'd held a position in market research. Returning to that work, she could quadruple her income while regaining her nights and weekends. She could.

She opened the email. It was an acceptance. Sonya had been accepted to a comparative literature program. Full funding for two years. A rural town across the country, known for heavy snowstorms. Star faculty. A small program that encouraged cross-departmental collaboration. Opportunity to apply for funding to study abroad. We were impressed with your writing sample and would love to have you.

The last email in Sonya's inbox was from the president of the university where she was an adjunct. He was saddened to inform the dear campus community that a faculty member had been found dead in her office in the Humanities building. Debra Polk, sixty-two years old, had contributed to the university's success for the past twenty-nine years. The university police chief said that the death appeared to have been the result of natural causes. Debra had no immediate family. Short-term counseling was available for employees, including adjunct instructors, through Life Matters, the university's employee assistance program. A 1-800 number was provided.

Spring break, Sonya thought. Debra's body must've stayed rotting behind the closed door of her office through the Spring break. Nobody, not a student, not a janitor, not a fellow faculty member, had approached the door of her office in that time.

Sonya went for that bottle of wine and poured herself a glass. Debra Polk's death was Debra Polk's death, and was it so bad? Lots of people died doing their jobs, the jobs that they loved. Sonya's life was Sonya's life. She and Debra Polk had little in common.

Helen More's Suicide

IN MEMORY OF PROFESSOR CAROLYN GOLD HEILBRUN

My retired colleague Marguerite called to tell me of Helen More's suicide. "Of all the sad, ludicrous things people do to themselves!"

She invited me over. "Thursday night, as usual. I could use the company of younger people."

It had been about a year since I'd first been invited to these Thursdays—monthly literary and musical soirees Marguerite hosted in her living room. Helen had been a regular at Marguerite's for several decades; the two women were close contemporaries and each a celebrity in her own field. Helen was a scholar of the English Romantics at the same university where Marguerite had taught Flaubert, Zola, and Balzac, and where I was now a junior faculty member in the English department. I'd heard of Professor More long before I met her: she lectured at the university from the 1960s until being forced into retirement in 2006, ostensibly due to age. She had a reputation as a militant feminist who eagerly engaged in battles about appointments and promotions, and her politics could have had something to do with it.

"Are they sure it was a suicide?" In person Helen was a quiet, reticent woman with a sly, sarcastic sense of humor, and the idea that she might've ended her own life seemed outlandish. Vague murder scenarios floated in my mind. A disgruntled student? A male professor, passed over for promotion years ago and blaming her for his career failure?

"Yes, quite. The details are unpleasant, but do you know what she wrote in her suicide note?"

"Of course she left a note."

"She said, 'This history is brought to its appointed close,' a quote from Wordsworth, I believe. 'Love to all.'"

I couldn't help laughing.

"Yet when you think that having written that, she took all those pills and put a plastic bag over her head," Marguerite's voice broke. "Anyway, it's not a conversation to have over the telephone. Do come over."

On Thursday afternoon, having collected the student papers after the last exam of the semester, I took the subway down to Greenwich Village. Marguerite lived on a third floor walk-up, in a wonderfully spacious and tall-ceilinged apartment that back in the 1970s she and her husband had converted from a pillow factory.

Since her husband's death ten years earlier, the apartment had slowly turned into a trap for Marguerite. She suffered from arthritis in her hands, shoulders, and knees, and walking up and down the stairs became a nearly impossible exercise. She ventured out once or twice a week with the assistance of a visiting nurse. The place could easily fetch three or four million dollars, and Marguerite could use the money. She was reluctant to sell. "I'd rather go without bread than without my piano and my books," she insisted.

A feeling of reverence and trepidation caught my breath as I climbed the stairs to her apartment. One never knew what kind of celebrity of the arts or music world could show up on any given Thursday. In her lifetime, Marguerite had known everyone, from Sartre and de Beauvoir to Picasso and Chagall. In the last few years, the circle of her acquaintances seemed to shrink, but nevertheless world-renowned musicians, poets, and playwrights sometimes appeared among her former colleagues and students.

I rang the doorbell and waited for several minutes as Marguerite crept to the door. "I'm afraid you're my only guest tonight," she said through the door, struggling with the lock and the knob. Finally, she pushed the door open. "Several people cancelled because of the end of the semester, and then, of course, there's the funeral. But come in, come in—we'll talk of that later."

She led me into the living room, heavily shaded from the street and dimly lit with two floor lamps. Decorated with musical instruments, piles of books on the floor and on the low tables, and bright modernist watercolors on the walls, the room seemed to belong to a royal palace, a vast, untouchable space. Usually Helen or one of Marguerite's older friends was on hand Thursday afternoons to help set up the room and the table for the evening. My host seemed eager enough to see me, yet being one-on-one with her made me unsure of any movement or gesture. "I do appreciate you coming tonight," she said. "You can't know how important the company of young people is at my age."

Having turned thirty-nine the past January, I had not thought of myself as "young" for a long time, but in the presence of Marguerite, who was some forty years my senior, I practically became a schoolgirl.

"Helen's funeral was today, and our friends asked me to attend, but I couldn't. It's physically difficult to arrange, and I'm too upset with Helen."

"I didn't know," I said, clearing my throat and blushing. Like a proper schoolgirl, I hadn't even thought to inquire about the funeral. And now in Marguerite's solemn presence, I felt as if I were trespassing in the temple of high suffering with no right to console my host.

"It's the loneliness that gets to you, I suppose," she said quietly, looking somewhere past me into the shadowy expanse of the room. "Helen lived such an active life, always fussing about her students, and when they pushed her into retirement—that was a blow."

"She didn't seem depressed. The poems she wrote were always so funny . . . . And that book of essays she was putting together, everyone looked forward to that."

"She kept herself busy. But who knows? If one could only see into another person's soul." Marguerite's glance focused on me, and with a slight shake of the head, she changed the topic. "Make yourself comfortable—I'll leave you for a moment to make the tea."

She shuffled toward the kitchen, and I started after her, meaning to help, as I'd seen the older women do, but Marguerite stopped me. "Feel free to look at the books, or to play something—I don't remember, do you play?" She wanted to do what she could without assistance, and I felt too shy to insist.

I could barely pick my way through "Frère Jacques" on the piano, so I sat down in my usual spot, on the sofa in front of a low table, luxuriating in the comforts of the room. The piano occupied a position of honor in the middle of her salon, a floor harp stood near the balcony window, and several violins and fiddles hung from a rack on the wall. I recalled my first night in this room, when having first learned of my interest in modernist poetry, a colleague in the French department invited me to come to a Thursday, warning that each guest was called upon to recite something by heart, no matter the language. That night more than twenty people, students and professors alike, spread over the sofas, or directly on the well-worn carpet between piles of books and musical instruments. Once upon a time, Marguerite, they told me, used to hold her choir practice here, and she'd played with several different chamber ensembles over the years.

Across from me, on a similar sofa on the other side of the low table, Helen More had sat only a few weeks ago, telling Marguerite about her son. I had arrived somewhat earlier than usual and so became a witness to this rather private conversation between the two women. Her son, Helen explained, lived in Tokyo with his wife and children and made a good deal of money as a marketing consultant to a large corporation. "He blew into town for a few days, on business, and offered to take me out to a Michelin-starred restaurant," Helen said. "He was running late after a business meeting and couldn't advise whether I should wait to eat. So I had a little dinner. At eight p.m., he finally came home, insisting he would take me out. An adult son must be obeyed."

"Did you enjoy the food?" Marguerite asked. She herself seemed to exist only on bread and cheese and fruit, and thin ginger biscuits she dunked in her tea. I could hardly imagine her eating more than a morsel of her meal, no matter the restaurant. Helen had a bulk about her stomach and thighs, though she was hardly overweight, and she looked particularly youthful and energetic that night, dressed as she was in jeans and sporting a new, spiky and fashionable haircut.

"I'm a farmer's daughter," Helen said. "My father kept milk cows and an apple orchard in Connecticut, a hard life, especially in the winter. We were taught to clean our plates."

Marguerite pushed the biscuit tin toward the middle of the table. Both she and I waited for Helen to continue. "Do you remember A. A. Milne?" Helen said, her expression changing and lips spreading in a quick smile. " 'James James Morrison Morrison Weatherby George Dupree took great care of his mother, though he was only three.' Robert loved this poem when he was little."

I hadn't heard the poem before, and upon request, she recited the whole thing. A kind of playful formality presided during those evenings: eventually each story had to lead to a poem. The muse governed all.

Recalling this episode now, weeks later, I imagined I had glimpsed in it the difference between the two women. Where Marguerite was steady in her habits and actively cultivated pleasure from her relationships, more inwardly-turned Helen hid her disappointments behind a sarcastic attitude and an air of mystery. But how did one get from that anecdote about her son to suicide?

Marguerite appeared in the hallway, carrying an elegant silver tray with teacups and biscuits. I stood to meet her and noticed that her hands shook and that she'd spilled half of the tea onto the saucers and the tray itself. "May I help you?" I offered again, at the risk of upsetting her by drawing attention to her ailments.

"Please." She handed me the tray. "There's more hot water in the kitchen, and some mandarin oranges. Would you be so kind to bring them here? I'm not feeling myself today."

I did as she asked and, as inconspicuously as possible, added a few table offerings I'd brought: a baguette and a wedge of aged brie. Marguerite was a great connoisseur of cheese, but the expense had grown too extravagant for her, I'd recently discovered.

"I think she did it because she was afraid of becoming like me," Marguerite said, when we were both settled at the table. She looked at her hands, lying limp and twisted on her lap.

"But you have such a beautiful life!"

Marguerite shivered, her back curving slightly toward the table. In the four weeks I hadn't seen her, she seemed to have aged a great deal, to have grown smaller and weaker. "Most of the time, yes," she said. "But I'm afraid Helen witnessed some of my darker moods."

"I know that you're in pain and that certain things are becoming increasingly difficult." I hastened to correct my impulsive comment.

Marguerite continued, "Helen was a great believer in the control over her destiny. That came from her politics, or maybe her politics originated from this kind of inner determination—I wonder. She looked at what was happening to me with a kind of horror. What? I was no longer interested in making the trip to Lincoln Center? Not even in a cab? I could no longer stay at the piano for more than five minutes? Music was everything to you, she used to say to me, as though I'd somehow forgotten that."

Everyone who'd known Marguerite before illness and her husband's death was full of fascinating stories about her. She'd been the heart of every social and artistic gathering well into her middle age. Her friends loved to recall those days, but Marguerite herself rarely alluded to that era, preferring to live in the present. The only regret she ever expressed was her loss of the ability to travel to France, to visit her daughter who lived there, to see the house where she'd lived during the war.

"There was no soothing Helen," Marguerite recollected. "And, frankly, I found the conversation upsetting. She once told me that when her mother was dying of cancer, she helped her to end things. I wondered then whether she was suggesting this route for me, and offering her assistance. A lot of people these days find nothing wrong with euthanasia for medical reasons, but there was something so very cold and rational about Helen's attitude to life."

I dropped the biscuit I was dunking into my tea. "Are you saying that Helen More killed her mother?"

"She never said so directly, but her hints were quite clear. Don't be horrified, dear. Or, rather, the horror comes from the fact that in Helen's mind, she acted with absolute rationality and mercy," Marguerite said, looking up at me. "What's the point of living after one has accomplished everything she wanted to? Helen devoted her life to fighting inherited traditions; she believed in controlling her destiny to the end. In the old days, our parents soldiered on because they felt needed, because they possessed a tremendous sense of obligation. My mother, even after her stroke, continued to knit socks for us and tried to mend our clothes. She couldn't sit or stand without help, and yet I felt I could leave my eight-year-old Valerie with her for a few hours. Our children don't have the same use for us; in that Helen was right."

The uncharacteristically flat and brusque tone of Marguerite's voice made me realize that she was probably speaking from that private dark mood to which she had alluded earlier. My parents were both still living and in good health, and I had never been forced to seriously consider the idea of assisted suicide. The rationality Marguerite described made my hair stand on end.

I wanted to say or do something to reassure her, but the words seemed too placid and devoid of meaning. The unconventional decorum of the room prevented me from moving closer to Marguerite and embracing her or holding her hand in mine. I cut off a piece of the baguette and smeared some cheese on it, offering her the open-faced sandwich. "Thank you," she said, smiling kindly, as I made another slice for myself.

"There's much to be said for living for the everyday pleasures," I said cautiously.

"A difficult concept to accept for us of the old world." Marguerite shook her head. "In that regard, Helen was very puritanical, like her ancestors. A life of pleasure was for her a life of no value—I know how Helen thought. I advised her to take some guest lecturing posts, to mentor some of her younger colleagues, to stay in touch. She did try once or twice to give talks around town, but I guess that wasn't enough. She was used to teaching large classrooms."

She let out a heavy sigh and fell silent. I had taken a rather large bite of the bread and cheese while she was talking, and for a while the room was filled with nothing but the sound of my jaws masticating. Startlingly, a grandfather clock chimed loudly from the hallway, and the violins and the harp responded to it with vibration. For a moment, the room resonated with music. "This silliness of Helen's has been terribly distressing, but we better talk of something else," Marguerite said, her tone lifting. "Tell me, what have you been working on?"

But before I could say anything, she interrupted me. "Wait, wait, I do have a funny Helen story I should tell you. Unlike most of our friends, you're young enough to appreciate it. About two years ago, Helen broke her arm, and the surgery went badly. They had to insert some metal into her bones to ensure that they grew together properly; a follow-up operation was scheduled. Helen suffered from a good deal of pain and complained constantly. So one of her former students brought her a batch of funny cookies—do you know what I mean?"

I nodded, surprised at the direction this story was taking.

"The student warned her not to eat more than a bite at a time, but the pain made Helen impatient, and she ate more than she should've. This was just before one of our poetry evenings—forgive me, I can't recall whether you were here or not. She recited a piece of Wordsworth's "Prelude" that day, and I noticed that she was much too amused by that utterly humorless poem. Of course, she was the specialist, and everyone trusted her interpretation. No one suspected a thing.

"She called me the next day and confessed what had happened. 'I had a revelation,' she declared. 'By the time I got to your door, I was so *high*, as the kids say, I didn't think I could construct a single sentence. And then it dawned on me—guess what? People are only self-conscious about themselves; nobody gives a hoot about you. If you've read as many Romantics and Victorians as I have in my lifetime, you might fool yourself into thinking that everyone's acutely aware of the behavior of others, constantly observing the smallest clues. Bullshit, pardon the expression! At seventy-six, I suddenly understood what my mother tried to explain when I was sixteen: Nobody cares! As long as you keep your mouth shut and stick to reflecting back their own thoughts, I said to myself, they wouldn't have a clue that something was amiss.' That was her big revelation." Marguerite concluded, "Giving it some thought, I had to admit there was truth to it. Nobody suspected a thing, including me. I was too busy playing a hostess to really pay attention to Helen, to question what about that pompous poem amused her so."

"Do you think that experience affected her final decision?" I asked.

"Who knows?" Marguerite said, her smile disappearing again. "All I know is that I had no sense of this coming, even though she and I talked nearly every day. I asked other friends, and nobody suspected anything. Helen was right in this, too: we're prisoners of our own minds."

The way she uttered that phrase sent a chill down my spine. "I hope you don't feel guilty or anything," I said. "You were a good friend to her. I'm sure she knew that."

"Oh no, I certainly have nothing to feel guilty about. But I do see Helen's point clearly. The death of an old woman cannot even be properly called tragic. It's expected. She remained in control to her very last breath—at least, one hopes she did. I'm left to wonder what prevents all of us, especially someone in a situation similar to mine, from following her example? At times, I'm tempted, I'm very tempted," Marguerite concluded, with a fierce look in her eyes, as if daring me to say something to contradict her.

I was speechless, sitting in front of her, pinned to the cushions by her stare, my heart a stone in my throat. Did Marguerite mean what she'd said? I had no reason to doubt her, and yet the statement contradicted the feelings she'd expressed earlier. No matter how much I wished to reassure her, or to say something positive, I couldn't do it under that heavy gaze. I felt utterly out of my depth.

Eventually Marguerite looked away, releasing me, and the conversation flowed along its more usual routes. She asked about my work, and I shared some ideas for the essay I was planning to write that summer. There was no line of poetry spoken that evening, and nothing else uttered about Helen More.

As we exchanged goodbyes, I walked to the door, waiting while she slowly followed me. Out on the landing, I listened as she bolted the two locks behind me, and after I heard the second click, ran down the three flights of stairs, anxious to be outside in the warm spring evening. I was going back uptown, to Spanish Harlem, to the apartment I shared with two women my age, both of them young business professionals, struggling to make ends meet in the city.

I felt life vibrating in every pore of my body. They sang and pulsed with the noises of the city, the rattling of the truck over the metal grates in the asphalt, the hum of the crowd at a nearby bar, up above a radio playing U2, and further on, outside my range of hearing, the clanging of the subway, the swishing of the Hudson, the horns of barges heading out to sea. All that waited for me, ready to accept me in its embrace, and at that moment I felt nothing but relief at leaving Marguerite's. It was as though the sounds of the street roused me from being buried alive in that house filled with disused musical instruments and treasured but unusable remnants of the past.

I let the rush of life sweep me off my feet and nearly skipped all the way to the subway station, but when I reached it, I stopped short, before descending the stairs. The humid air and the stench of something rotting emerging from down below brought home the ugly and depressing reality of Helen More's death, sucking air out of my chest, anchoring me to the dirty pavement. The image of her body underground, decomposing and crawling with maggots, felt so vivid that I passed the subway station and headed toward the river, hoping for some relief. Helen More ended her life, and the students' papers in my bag weighed heavily on my shoulder, the myriad of meaningless tasks and unfulfilled desires separating me from the end of that night, that week, the end of my life. I thought of splurging on a cab, but after a second thought, could not justify the expense. I turned around and walked back to the subway.

Dandelion

A story Oz had written nearly won a prize. Though the story came in second, it received some notice. A New York agent contacted her. "I have read the story of yours and think it's wonderful. Do you have a novel you need representation for?"

Oz had no novel, but she did have a nineteen-month-old. "He's very much like a novel," she told the agent. "Can I ship him to you? People are telling me, since he can walk, that he's no longer a baby. Soon he'll be ready for publication."

The agent asked to see a picture. Oz sent a recent image of the child in the park, holding a white-headed dandelion by the stem. The child's pale curls, backlit by the setting sun, resembled the dandelion.

The agent liked the picture and asked to see "Dandelion" in person.

Before shipping her child off to New York, Oz added the final touches. She cut his hair and trimmed his nails. She gave him a long bath to scrub the dandruff from his scalp and the playground grime from his hands and face. She outfitted him with a leash harness, so he wouldn't be able to run into traffic. She cut off feet from his pajamas and straps from his hat to make it look more like a baseball cap. She taught him to smile and give high-fives when he was too shy to say hello. Oz didn't have time to teach him to use the toilet, and this concerned her a great deal. She wrote to the agent, asking for advice, but the agent assured her it would be fine. If a publisher would take "Dandelion" on, they would toilet-train using their preferred method. "I frequently advise authors to leave one obvious flaw for the publisher to edit," the agent wrote. "The editors will edit, and unless you give them something obvious to work with, they are liable to start messing with the parts they better leave alone."

Having done everything she could think of, Oz presented the child to her husband. Her husband was Oz's first reader, and though not very familiar with the publishing industry, gave common sense advice that helped her make sure she was on the right track. "You may have cut his hair too short," the husband said, running his fingers across the child's head. "Otherwise, he's perfect." He asked the child to point out his belly button and then tickled him until the child was squealing with laughter. "I'm going to miss him," the husband said. "But I guess if he's to be published, I'll see him soon."

The husband helped Oz package and ship "Dandelion" to New York.

Then, they waited.

The agent acknowledged receipt, and said that "Dandelion" was as beautiful in person as he'd looked in the picture.

A week later, she wrote to say that he was a very active child with boundless curiosity, and that she would right away introduce him to several publishers and schedule an auction. She asked if there were a code word or a particular bedtime routine that could help "Dandelion" relax and be still for more than a few minutes at a time. Reading books to him didn't seem to help; he wanted to flip the pages himself and kept asking to see the cats. "I'm not sure what cats he means. These old school publishers are tired," she wrote. "They want to take on familiar, well-behaved projects."

Oz suggested taking "Dandelion" on a good long walk, to tire him out, and then giving him a bath.

When she didn't hear back from the agent, she started to worry.

After three weeks, Oz broke decorum and wrote again to ask about "Dandelion." "He's my only child," she explained, "and, though I know it's already out of my hands, I do worry about his future. I want to make sure I've done my best by him."

It took the agent another week to write back. "Dandelion" had been introduced to nearly a dozen publishers, the agent reported, but unfortunately, he failed to make the right impression. It turned out, he didn't do well under pressure. He kept asking for mommy and other things he couldn't have. He didn't respond well to discipline. He refused to hold hands when walking down the street and darted into traffic with such force that he took his leash with him. He was still alive, but barely.

In short, no bids were forthcoming. The agent didn't see any point in trying again later. A basic character flaw made the child unacceptable to the major publishers. "Being in San Francisco," the agent wrote, "you will be tempted to publish with an independent press. I would strongly counsel against this. Publishing with a small press makes you look desperate and abstruse. If you want to make it in New York, you have to work harder."

The agent sent the child back. Oz barely recognized him. He looked like a dandelion whose seeds had all blown away. He smelled like a sewer; his loaded diaper had not been changed during transit but instead encased in a second pair of pants.

Together, Oz and her husband washed the child. They'd hoped that once his hair was clean and dry, it would curl back up, but they were disappointed. The awful smell was gone, but the hair remained thin and straight.

Oz returned to writing short fiction, while her husband cared for the child. "Let's see if you still like being tickled," he said, and chased after the boy, who promptly climbed from the dining room chair onto the table, nearly turning both over as he jumped to the floor. A step ahead of his father, he ran to his old bedroom, where Oz had recently moved her desk, and went to hide in her drawer.

Stroller Selection

The choices were: pink black white orange and blue. Orange, she thought, was the color of sunrises gerbera lions fire. Goldfish were orange, the plain and the talking kind. The couch in the apartment where at eighteen she rented a room had been orange. She'd rescued it from a dumpster and later the man she'd been worshipping crouched on it next to her and penetrated her with his finger his penis while she said no no no no wordlessly, too awed by the improbability of what was happening by the magnitude of consequences to complain of pain or even to figure out what was happening: penis? finger? two fingers? thumb? She recalled the schemata of sperm entering an egg and the word abortion and the words herpes gonorrhea HIV syphilis in the time it took him to grow tired bored done and roll off her. He never noticed the blood on the orange couch; at the time, she felt grateful for that. In the subsequent years, more fingers followed, and more thumbs.

*   *   *

The white stroller was discounted, and she nodded when her husband called it, white.

Falling Violently Ill Beneath the Torrey Pines

It takes the sudden increase of only . . . who knows how many degrees, in Fahrenheit . . . in the body temperature's set-point. The body creaks on its bones, the arms and legs distended, sore from having scrubbed the deck, the rug of the hotel room after the vomiting toddler; the vertebrae of the lower back feel as though they have fused and ossified.

And as the whole anchors: Thank you grass for being there, Thank you sun and wind for being so Californian, Thank you virus for taking us in turns—the toddler is doing better and the husband will be sick tomorrow.

The mind sets sailing, it sprints billowed by the clarinet music from the car radio and the swarm of mosquitos rising from the grass and the moments of leisure stolen from the Google calendar to straighten these crooked Torrey pine limbs into the masts of hundred-year-old Karelian pines not actually seaworthy, badly used by time, weather-beaten, whose swaying swaying presided over the weeks the months the years of fever-ridden escape fantasies.

My home being too dark too barren, the soil too cold too sandy with too much clay, to grow peaches plums pears tomatoes sunflowers human offspring into human beings, and so spawning roots as the branches of the Torrey pines, craggy and twisted through sand through clay through naked feet through oceans and continents so that only a slight fever reveals their ossified clawing.

I'm sorry my baby you who are sick and I'm hollow.

Legacy

Vacation, their first since Jones's birth. Hawaii. Robin, Lesley, and their children Milo and Jones are at sea, on a boat with the glass floor, looking at fish. Robin checks work email on her phone.

Her boss is furious that she hasn't responded to an email from a prospective legacy student about enrolling for the fall semester. An annual contribution of two-and-a-half-million dollars is at stake. The boss threatens to deduct that sum from Robin's salary. The threat isn't real, but the frustration is. If Robin were laid off, that would just about do them in. Between the increase in their monthly mortgage payments and the purchase of the Subaru after the Prius died, she and Lesley just make ends meet.

So what's the problem? Lesley asks. Milo repeats, What's your problem, Mommy?

The legacy student has limped through a few semesters at a community college, with a grade point average of 2.35, and there's no way in hell, legacy or not, she could enroll at the university without showing more effort.

How long have you been sitting on this email? Lesley asks.

I don't know. More than a month.

Robin has been working the same job for sixteen years and she really, really should know better. She does.

Is that a lot? Jones asks.

A month, Milo says. That's like thirty Oreos.

Reese's are my favorite.

Don't you write these types of letters all the time? Thanks for the money, but there's nothing we can do?

It's different now. My boss is under pressure from the VP to raise money. I've told you this before. Annual givers are valuable. I'm supposed to be cultivating these relationships.

Lesley is silent. Robin stares at the glass panel under her feet. The water is a perfect aquamarine color but it's murky. They'd been sold on the opportunity to glimpse sea turtles, dolphins, tropical fish, shipwrecks, and living coral reefs, but a recent storm had raised sand from the ocean's floor. Robin should've known better than booking a boat based on a gimmick. The kids, tired of sitting, long have had a better idea, and are standing by the boat's railing to look out from the side of the boat. Lesley joins them.

Look, Mama! A turtle! A real life turtle!

Two turtles!

Two turtles and one of them is looking at me!

Thirty turtles!

That's three, Lesley corrects. Let's count. One, two—

Thirty, shouts Jones. I saw thirty turtles!

Do you have to think about this now? Tonight, we'll put the kids to bed, and I can help you craft that email.

I want to help Mommy, Milo says. I can dictate. You should say, Thank you for your generous donation. The university students really appreciate it. However—

Robin's eyes tear up.

Milo! That's great, Milo, Lesley says. You can compose my letters for me.

Thank you for your donation, Jones repeats, a look of authority on his face. Look! More turtles! That's thirty.

Robin feels the warm breeze on her skin, but shivers. She has no energy to join Lesley and the kids at the railing, and stares through the bottom of the boat. Occasionally, she can see a shape of a large fish swimming below. The notion of legacy has obviously lulled the student into a false sense of security. If Robin were to do her job right, she would write such an email that would inspire the young woman to take ownership in her life, to go back to the community college and pull off a couple of As. Then, Robin could help her with the transfer credits. Composing the email, Robin needed to imply all this without making any promises. There was nothing she could do for the student if she didn't even try.

This email should be easy.

Her boss, Robin thinks, is working through August. She pictures the tall gray updo, shaking slightly as her boss drinks cup after cup of tea in her corner cubicle, alone or nearly alone on the whole second floor of the admissions building. Her boss is sixty-three. How long will she be able to stave off retirement? It had been many years since Robin had aspired to rise in the department.

Robin marks the email from her boss unread. She owes her a phone call, but the difference in time zones makes a phone call difficult. Tonight. She will deal with this tonight, after the kids go to sleep and she and Lesley settle on the little balcony of their hotel room. Robin will look at the stars, drink wine, and type fast.

Email

At this juncture in my career, my inbox has become the fossil preserve for good ideas. Fortunately, most fossils are not rare, and the public is allowed to collect specimens no larger than the size of their palms. By which I mean that I can delegate most of my tasks so the urgent correspondence is shuffled out of the way. But if a request comes in that requires the slightest degree of initiative, a spark of creative, original thought, that letter turns into a stegosaurus and has to wait its turn to be interned in a museum.

One's Share

One has a child with one's partner, a shared child, only to learn that the relationship with one's child is individual, solely one's own. The partner's relationship with the child has little bearing, and only indirectly, on one's own relationship with the child. The partner does make the child laugh. That can be shared. A good laugh—and then back to one's own solitude, now with the child.

My Mother at the Shooting Range

My mother was born in Leningrad, after the Great Patriotic War. When she was seven years old, she became addicted to shooting practice. The range was housed in the basement of the five-story residential building where she lived. The basement, a remodeled air-raid shelter, was a long, low-ceilinged room, filled with cigarette smoke and the smell of stale beer. My mother frequented the place on her way home from first grade. One rainy September evening, my grandmother came home after a long shift at the chemical plant to find her daughter missing. The sun had long set, and everyone in the apartment building had settled into their supper. Women were washing the dishes; men read the newspaper out loud. My grandmother ran up and down five flights of unlit, foul-smelling stairs, knocking on the doors, interrogating the neighbors: Have you seen my little girl? Black hair, two braids, brown coat. Please ask your children, have they seen Masha today? Are they sure? Do you know anyone who might have seen her?

My grandfather returned home from the machine-building factory and planted himself in front of the telephone, methodically calling the school, the hospital, the police department, the morgue. My grandmother put her boots back on and, with her coat unbuttoned and the shawl trailing behind her, flew all the way to the school and back, walked into every open store, opened the doors to every dark staircase, searched every blind alley and courtyard, called, "Masha, Masha!" until her voice collapsed and the name choked up her throat. My grandfather wouldn't leave the apartment: somebody had to be home in case the police brought Masha back. Finally, an hour or two later, a drunk shuffled from the basement and, making his way to his own apartment on the top floor, stumbled upon my grandmother, her hands fisted and her face white, sitting on the step in front of the door to her apartment. The man wiped his nose and mouth with the back side of his hand and, slurring the words together, managed to express half a thought about the basement, the range, and two braids helping to load air guns with lead pellets.

My mother describes in detail the metal dishes, dented at the bottom and around the edges, where the pellets were measured, ten, twenty, fifty per person. Coarse hands take off the work gloves, grope the steel muzzle, crack it in half, and stuff a tiny shell full of unbound potential into a barren, meaningless hole. Sometimes, the thick, sweaty fingers miss, and the pellet escapes, drops to the floor, rolls under the counter, where the smell of beer is particularly strong. The hands hug the two lengths of the rifle so tightly their knuckles go white, they jerk the broken rod back together—and the gun is complete again, the magic is locked within! The man jams the wooden butt of the rifle, polished by the shoulders of the men before him, between his own neck and shoulder. His movement is swift, so swift that it makes him uncomfortable, and he spends some time adjusting the gun, clearing his throat, shifting his weight from one leg to another. Finally, he leans forward, plants his elbow on the counter so firmly that the counter shakes, presses his eye, his entire face, to the crude metal sight and takes his aim. What target will he choose? Will he hit the mark?

At the top of the back wall, painted sky blue, the metallic gray ducks with yellow noses are flying. They carry the largest targets, the easiest to hit, but to win another round—another set of pellets—one must shoot all of them, reloading the gun each time. Not many amateur marksmen are capable of that, and only a few are interested in trying. There are other targets to choose from. The windmills produce the best effect: their blades spin and sputter the longest. The brown squirrels and the fluffy white rabbits fall down with a loud clatter but altogether less to-do. The man must choose the target fast: the space at the counter is filling up, and if he hesitates to shoot for too long, his neighbor might try for the same target. Still, he takes a swig of beer, adjusts his belt, and pats the head of the little girl who is waiting for him to shoot. He has half-a-dozen pellets left, and if he wants them to last through the night, each shot must be weighted out and carefully planned. A miss incites a string of curses, a nasty spatter through his teeth, an angry kick of the rifle butt against the cement floor; the metal dish with the few remaining pellets is hurled hard against the wall. He leans down to pick up one of the pellets, and notices the little girl again, and apologizes. Pardon my French, he says, but this fucking windmill is going to die.

My mother stares at the row of men without blinking. She stands on her tiptoes, squishing her nose on top of the roughly polished counter. One of the black braids has come undone, the white sateen ribbon has slipped away, lost. She is mesmerized by the movements of the men's hands, by the fireworks of sounds, by the repeated spectacle of victory and failure. She makes friends with the lucky ones, those who smile and wink at her, who try to impress her with their technique, to share with her some part of their success. A man shoots! Oh, the moment of pure joy, the unadulterated happiness—the bunny jumps a short distance, falls head first into the trough, makes a clacking noise, raises its tail into the air. The bunny is down, defeated, subdued. That's happiness produced directly by human hands, with practice and skill, with patience and per-severance. This man has taken a risk, has spent his last shell, has made a shot, and is rewarded. He doesn't need to go home quite yet, the evening can continue. He drinks down his beer and waits for his dish to be refilled with pellets. He asks for my mother's name and wants to know what grade she's in at school. My mother performs a service: she collects the pellets from the floor and surreptitiously redistributes them between the men. She favors the winners, the ones whose luck is running strong, and has no pity for the men who have not been able to hit a single duck.

In our childhood, we were all Buddhists, my mother says at the end of her story. Our goals were simple, our pleasures were pure. She says this—her voice on the telephone sounds wistful and tender—and immediately switches subjects: so, when are you going to have a baby? It's time, she says. The longer you wait, the harder it will be. If you're afraid, have a baby sooner rather than later. It's your duty to your father and me, she says. You can give birth and then let us raise the child. We'll take care of it, I'll take care of it, she says. We'll pay for a nanny, she says, we'll babysit ourselves. Think how much happiness a baby brings, she says. Don't be selfish.

There Will Be Dragons

A small toddler has fallen into the sandpit, and suddenly there's blood everywhere. The young nanny rushes to him. "Are you okay, baby? Are you okay?"

My eighteen-month-old daughter and I are the only other people present. The sun is barely up. My daughter woke up at 5:35 in the morning and hasn't been able to go back to sleep. We've just arrived and are lingering by the stroller, unpacking our sand toys.

"Baby. Waaa-waaa," my daughter says, looking up at me. We know this boy, a month or two younger than my daughter. He and his nanny frequent this playground in the early mornings.

The boy is crying. The nanny lifts him from the sand and holds him close, trying to assess what's happened. Her nails are painted a shiny red, I notice. The color offsets that of the blood. Blood is brighter.

The boy's head is fine, his eyes, his nose. The blood is gushing from his mouth. The nanny presses on his jaws, sticks a finger in the back of his mouth. "Open! Open!" she repeats. His instinct is to clamp down. There's too much blood to see the wound.

Keeping one hand on my daughter's shoulder, I stand still. I've come a long way in learning to parent in the past months, but the unexpected leaves me baffled.

The boy stops crying and gives a kind of a yawn. He has no front teeth. Is he teething or did his brand new teeth just break? I finger the phone in my pocket. Should I call the ambulance? I don't want to interfere in another woman's business. That nanny probably has a lot more experience

40

with children than I do. She is also a lot younger. My mind's so sluggish I can hear it churning.

"Do you need help?" When I finally push out the question, my voice sounds squeaky.

"There's too much blood in his mouth," the nanny says. "Could you hand me that water bottle?"

"Bluh," my daughter says. She's been repeating everything.

The nanny wrestles the boy into the stroller, pours water into his mouth. He swallows some, spits some up. He has a curious expression, as if listening to his own body. He then sees the blood on his hands, on his jacket, on the nanny's hands. His eyes grow big and his mouth opens. The tears come flooding. There's more blood.

"Bluh," my daughter repeats and points at the nanny's white shirt, spotted with red. How does my eighteen-month-old know what blood looks like? I'm glad she's figured it out and I won't need to explain.

She pushes against my embrace, wanting to go to the boy. I hold her back. I have no idea what's going through her mind at this moment. "Don't worry," I tell her. "That child's hurt, but he'll be okay."

Maneuvering the stroller toward the playground exit, the nanny tells me, "We'll go home and call his mother."

"You should call the doctor," I tell her. I doubt the nanny's been able to get a good look inside his mouth. What if the child swallowed something? What if the blood is a symptom of an internal injury?

My daughter runs after them and, when the gate closes, grips the bars. "Bye-bye," she yells after the child. An idea dawns on me. Something must've hurt the child, and it could be still there, hiding in the sandbox. My daughter's still attached to the fence as I steal away to survey the sand-pit for glass, sharp sticks, broken toys.

I find nothing. But that doesn't mean there is nothing there.

When I look up, I see my daughter engaged with a large dog. The dog is sniffling her through the rods of the fence. The breed's terrifying, but my baby lets the dog lick her face and fingers, giggling. "Bluh," she says. The dog yawns, baring its teeth.

That's it. I pick up my daughter and, despite her cries of protest, buckle her into her stroller. I have no idea where to take her, but, I hope, once I catch my breath, I'll think of something.

I glance at the phone. It's seven o'clock in the morning.

If You've Dreamt of a Jew

A childhood friend emailed me this link. "If you've dreamt of a Jew," the Russian-language webpage reads, "there's a scoundrel among your acquaintance, a person who's trying to destroy your reputation. Commingling with a Jew in your sleep promises a successful resolution of the difficult situation. The backstabbing person will be punished, and you will be properly rewarded for the job well done."

My friend still lives in the same town in Russia where she and I grew up and that I left twenty years ago. Eleven time zones separate us. I haven't seen her in a few years, and lately the communication between us has dwindled to birthday and New Year's greetings. She's assuming that life hasn't changed me much and that I still find Jewish jokes funny. I am to this day the only Jew she knows or thinks she knows well enough. I do not now nor have I ever practiced Judaism; if, in my Soviet passport, "Jewish" was listed as my "nationality," she, of all people, might remember how little meaning there was for me in this accident of my biography. I haven't even suffered for it.

In 1992, after the Soviet Union fell apart, and so many of the world's religious sects sent their proselytizers to the former republics, my friend and I made a sport of chatting up the clean-shaven young men and the sneaker-clad women who turned up in our town. Fifteen at the time, we hung out downtown, bought ourselves ice cream, and, trying to look sophisticated, arm in arm, circled the entrance to the hotel where foreign tourists stayed. Inevitably somebody stopped us to ask what life in Russia was like. We used the opportunity to practice our English. I thought at the time that my friend and I approached the proselytizers with the equal degree of cynicism, but it turned out that neither of us was quite cynical enough. A few years later, I emigrated to America, and my friend became an auditor at the Church of Scientology. Later, she graduated from scientology to the Russian orthodoxy. The last time I saw her, we got into an argument about the theory of evolution. She made fun of me for thinking humans came from monkeys. "Maybe you like to think that you come from monkeys," she said. "I don't." I'm still searching for the last word to end this argument with.

The site my friend has linked to is secular, but it's the sort of a secular site that religious people link to. "My Dreams is a contemporary dream interpretation guide. The World"—capitalized—"The World is changing with incomprehensible speed, and the subconscious mind reflects this rate of change. The classical guide to dreams lost its relevance. If you've dreamt of Coca-Cola, you won't find the interpretation of this image in a classical guide. As new objects enter our reality, our dreams become contemporized. My Dreams Guide is based on the most recent oneirological and psychological studies, as well as the research from cognitive neuroscience. The classic dreams are considered and contemporary interpretations provided."

I've read their interpretation of the Jew dream, and I can't unread it. I want to believe in humanity. I want to believe that when my friend decided to send me the link, she didn't mean for me to laugh at the Jew dream per se, but aimed at the more profound irony, as though saying, Look, we have the internet now, but the internet has become merely a new vehicle for dissemination of hate speech and prejudice. My friend was educated as a computer scientist and she knows, she must know, the difference between science and this. A chilling thought that I push to the back of my mind: Had she dreamed of me and gone online, looking for the interpretation?

According to My Dreams Guide, to dream of moving to America is an omen of an improving financial situation.

A conversation about religion in one's dream is a sign of anxiety, and also a sign of inner strength and ability to problem solve.

To dream of a friend is a bad sign, an indication of trouble to come at work or in school. To dream of a close friend is a sure sign of a looming tragedy.

The experience of perusing My Dreams Guide is not unlike being stuck in a recurrent nightmare: I've been here before, and I'm terrified and upset. Why does my psyche crave this fodder? Why can't I stop reading? At fifteen, living in the country that was recovering from the seventy years of totalitarian regime with the help of Anatoly Kashpirovsky, a television hypnotist whose healing séances came to be broadcast on Channel One alongside Disney cartoons, the country where financial pyramid schemes and stock market emerged in the same breath and where public discourse about religion had only recently become decriminalized, living in this post-Perestroika Russia, I had been as lost as everyone else. It has taken years of studying critical thinking to learn to distinguish knowledge from conspiracy theory and fact from prejudice. My friend, in the meantime, found Jesus.

I am tempted to copy and paste a message to my friend, "To dream of a close friend is a sign of tragedy." To give her the taste of the medicine she's given me. But I decide to sleep on it, and in the morning I write back, "I love you too." At the end of the line, I add a smiley face.

Rose's Mother

On the black-and-white photograph Rose has always kept next to her mattress, her mother is smoking in the hallway of the University library, and three-year-old Rose stands outside of her mother's reach, looking up at her face. Her mother is in her bell-bottom jeans and a trim sweater, under which her small breasts seem fuller and healthier than reality proved. Her bobbed hair is swept back, away from her face, and curls slightly up at the jawline. Rose imagines, rather than is able to recall, that her mother cut her own hair.

Her mother had been so cool. The coolest.

From the mattress in the loft above the tattoo parlor Rose moves to a sleeping bag in a tent out in the Forest Reserve, then to a bunk bed in a skiing lodge. She makes enough money to buy a computer. In these years, when she looks at the photograph, she focuses most keenly on the space between the mother and daughter, the foot or foot and a half that separated her three-year-old self from her mother. She tries to fill that space with books. French books, because her mother had been French.

She doesn't know what her mother made of the books she'd studied. Books, though, imposed their own imperatives. Rose is growing up. She's studying for her master's degree and is going to Haiti to teach English and study Creole literature. When she looks at the picture now, she notices the open door of a study hall, and that she stands on one side of that door, and her mother on the other.

Doctor Sveta

Doctor Sveta was twenty-six years old when the Navy commissariat summoned her to Leningrad and put her on a cargo ship among a motley crew of agronomists, agricultural engineers, livestock breeders, and tractor drivers, none of whom knew where the ship was headed or how long the journey might take. Her fellow passengers looked as confused at finding themselves confined to a seafaring vehicle as Doctor Sveta felt. No tractors accompanied them: not a cow, not even a single chicken. The agronomists and tractor drivers were healthy young men and a few women, two of them visibly pregnant. Doctor Sveta had been trained as a surgeon in Leningrad; she assumed it was in this capacity she'd been recalled from her post at a hospital in Minsk, Belarus. Besides the ship's medic, there were no doctors aboard and not even a basic medical facility. Doctor Sveta worried she'd have to embrace a crash course in obstetrics.

Half a century later, as she tells me this story, Doctor Sveta recalls the words of her professor from medical school, who had counseled her to spend a semester or two at an obstetrics ward. "The work's not glamorous, but necessary," this wizened World War II veteran told her. "I assure you, it won't hurt your own prospects as a mother." Doctor Sveta found the man's advice offensive. Did he direct his male students to obstetrics? She would be a surgeon.

She and I are sitting to one side of a banquet table, arranged with the other tables in a U-shape, in the basement space of a downtown St. Petersburg restaurant. It's my aunt's seventy-fifth birthday party, and in the last-minute seating arrangement, my family placed me next to Doctor Sveta, my aunt's friend from medical school. My mother's obstetrician, Doctor Sveta was the first person to hold my infant self in her arms. Every time I visit St. Petersburg from the United States, she's anxious to check up on me, to make sure I'm taking my vitamins and exercise in the mornings. Lately, my mother, my aunt, and nearly everyone I know in St. Petersburg has been concerned that although my husband and I have been married for several years, we don't have children yet. At first, people blamed my American husband for our decision to wait, but now that I'm in my mid-thirties, they don't know what to think. A few days ago, a near-perfect stranger—my mother's engineer colleague—handed me a piece of paper with a phone number on it. "Young women are suffering today from the birth control pills they'd been sold on. People come to this man from the United States for consultation all the time; he can give you a prescription that will work wonders," the woman said. I made a joke about this doctor being more up-to-date than modern medicine, but the woman pushed the paper into my hands, insisting, "Call him."

I'm half-expecting Doctor Sveta to add her voice to the choir. Tonight, in honor of my aunt's birthday, she drank a glass of sweet red wine and launched into her story. I'm doing my best to connect the dots.

"So where was that cargo ship heading?"

"I'll tell you. Listen—"

Doctor Sveta came from Mogilev, Belarus, where her mother worked as a technologist at a synthetic fiber plant. Her father, a Red Army officer, had been killed in the war Doctor Sveta calls "The Great Patriotic"—the Soviet moniker for World War II. In 1960, Doctor Sveta graduated from the First Medical Institute in Leningrad with a degree in surgery and a rank of Navy lieutenant. After graduation, she wanted to stay in Leningrad—"It seemed the center of the world for a provincial girl"—but to a non-resident, the jobs weren't forthcoming. Out-of-towners were generally perceived to be an unreliable and potentially dangerous element, and hospitals were afraid to take a chance. Some friends recommended a fictive marriage to secure a Leningrad address, but the young doctor decided to return to Belarus, to Minsk—closer to her mother, but not too close. She procured an assignment to a surgery ward of a teaching hospital.

Doctor Sveta seems to be blindsided by the memories of her youth that are flooding back at once, bringing up unexpected emotions. Her voice is starting to shake, and drops of moisture gather at the bottom of her translucent eyelids. Because she doesn't have family of her own to practice on, her stories are raw, they have not congealed into a series of neat, punchy anecdotes. In Minsk, Doctor Sveta says, the work was demanding, the hospital understaffed, and the equipment substandard. Some among her colleagues looked upon her surgical training with suspicion. Recent innovations with endoscopy and the integration of metallurgy and plastics into surgery—experiments she'd been fascinated by in Leningrad—were frowned upon in Minsk. This caused tension at first, but eventually the head of the department took her under his wing and let her assist on his cases.

Listening to her talk, I have to remind myself that the Leningrad of Doctor Sveta's youth and today's St. Petersburg are one and the same city. Contemporary St. Petersburg feels hopelessly backwards, at least as far as medicine is concerned. I'm an anesthesiology resident at Mass General in Boston, and after difficult shifts, I entertain myself by imagining what my life would've been like had I stayed in St. Petersburg. I recall the vomit-green walls and creaky wooden windows of the hospitals and the outpatient clinics, the smell of urine in the hallways, the waiting rooms packed with small children and the elderly, and I feel privileged to be going back to work at the efficiency and safety-protocol-obsessed American hospital.

"So, you were recalled to Leningrad to board that cargo ship? What then, Doctor Sveta?"

"In Minsk, I'd grown fond of kayaking. The hospital was close to the river, and I could go after work sometimes. It was a popular sport back then, and I was good at it. I was training with the men's team, and our coach was an Olympic champion. Who knows, maybe I could've been selected for the Olympic team, if things had turned out the way I dreamed."

I can easily believe this. Even now, in her seventies, Doctor Sveta is in good shape. She's not very tall but has broad shoulders and well-developed musculature. She's the only one of my aunt's graduating class who's still working and who never seems to have any health complaints. My aunt, for years an administrator of an outpatient clinic, retired three years ago after suffering a series of cardiac episodes. Two of their male classmates, both practicing surgeons, are already dead. The whole medical field that was barely holding together on the passion and dedication of the old guard is falling apart. As governmental subsidies give way to new commercial medicine and insurance schemes, Doctor Sveta is one of the few who still refuses to overcharge her patients and doesn't accept gifts larger than a box of chocolates. Her hospital salary barely puts food on her table. As she speaks, I can see two gaping holes on the right side of her upper jaw. She doesn't even have money for dentures.

She jumps to the subject of her mother, and the chronological momentum of her story gives way to nostalgia. What makes her narrative interesting are the vividly remembered details about a way of life and the country where I too had been born and that since has ceased to exist. Sometime after Doctor Sveta had settled in Minsk, her mother came from Mogilev for a visit. She shared Doctor Sveta's bed in the room she rented from a local family, and cooked a week's worth of thick potato soup with fatback and potato pancakes fried with pork and onions. With considerable pride, the then-young Doctor Sveta showed her mother around the hospital, a pre-revolutionary building gutted by the Nazis during the war and renovated in the 1950s. She introduced her mother to a few colleagues, and had a nurse take her mother's arterial pressure and draw blood for tests. "You should really cut down on starches, fat meats, and lard," the young doctor counseled her mother. "These will cause you to have a heart attack."

"The silly things we remember!" Doctor Sveta tells me. "I cherished the idea of taking my mother for a ride in a double-seated kayak, but it was drizzling and she refused. 'And you call yourself a doctor!' my mother said. 'You're a young woman, Sveta, and you should know better than to go near water in such weather—or you'll never be able to give birth.' This still counted as received wisdom in those days."

"In this, all mothers are alike," I complain, looking around. I'm not sure whether I want my mother to be within or without earshot of this conversation. Her seat is empty; she's on the other side of the room, managing the arrangement of microphones for the toasts. "I can't have a rational conversation with my parents about this anymore. They don't want to hear my arguments. I'm their daughter, and therefore, having children is my obligation to them."

"And they are right!" Doctor Sveta immediately switches sides. "Don't look at me—my life is not an example for anyone. There will come a time when you will want children more than anything, but it'll be too late. Your parents want only what's best for you."

From the beginning of this evening, when Doctor Sveta entered the restaurant, and my mother led her to the empty chair next to me, I've been feeling set up, like maybe my mother, or my aunt, or both of them asked Doctor Sveta to have "a talk" with me. Having exhausted their own arsenal of arguments about the necessity of children, they have turned to the resident expert on the matter and asked Doctor Sveta to use her influence. Here comes the lecture, finally, I think, and in the last attempt to divert it, appeal to her logic. "Is this how you thought when you were my age?"

"Oh no," Doctor Sveta sighs. "Like you, I was focused on my career, on my bright future as a surgeon. And kayaking! I dreamed about my own Olympic medal. There was no point in trying to explain any of that to my mother."

"Was this before or after you were summoned to the cargo ship?"

"I was summoned to Leningrad, and they even gave me a train ticket! But I didn't know what I was supposed to do there, or how long they'd keep me."

Leaving Minsk, Doctor Sveta prided herself on her resourcefulness, which expressed itself chiefly in thinking to bring a winter coat and the current issue of *Soviet Sport*. She had written a note to her landlady, asking the woman to hold onto her things. She explained her sudden departure as being "dispatched as a medic on a critical Naval mission of vital importance to the Soviet Union," hoping this would warrant the safekeeping of her old school books and clothes. She sent a telegram to her mother, which at the time she'd thought communicated all her mother needed to know. "Summoned to Leningrad. Will write soon." She soon regretted the terseness of her message. But by then, the ship was already at the far edge of the Baltic Sea, cut off from communication.

The toasts are starting. Luckily, I'm considered the baby of the family and so too young to have anything to say on this occasion. Older family members, colleagues, grateful patients, who over the years have become friends, each in turn receive the microphone and, with a champagne glass in hand, make speeches. Some read awkward form poems. "Every profession is needed / every profession is wanted / but most important of all / is yours, dear doctor." Etc. Some try to sing. My aunt stands up after every toast and theatrically hugs the speaker and his or her entire family, kisses each of them three times on the cheeks. I get a creepy feeling that she's saying good-byes.

Doctor Sveta declines when the microphone comes her way. She is not a public person, and until today, I've never heard her talk about herself. Instead, she whispers something into my aunt's ear and kisses her once. My aunt nods, and as she moves on, I see her wiping away a tear.

Once, when I was about five years old, my aunt took me to see Doctor Sveta at the hospital where she worked and where I'd been born. Visitors were not allowed in the obstetrics wards back then, but my aunt had connections with the hospital through her job and was a familiar face, so they let the two of us right in. We arrived as Doctor Sveta was preparing for delivery. When she came out to greet us, she was wearing a white gown, and her hands, as she reached down to hug me, were puffy and red. At that moment, she appeared to me as an evil dragon from folk tales that was going to snatch me away from my aunt and tear me to pieces. Doctor Sveta seemed all-powerful. She, who had given me life, might also take it away. I hid behind my aunt's skirt and, to the horror of the adults in the room, screamed as if my life depended on it. The newborns in the ward took my lead, raising such a havoc that my aunt and I were forced to flee.

I look at Doctor Sveta's hands as she takes a forkful of mashed potatoes, trying to glimpse what I'd seen in them as a child, that power of life and death. Now her hands are wrinkled and marked with splotches of discoloration. Her nails are cropped so close to the flesh, the tips of her fingers are flattened and sausage-like. It's much easier to picture Doctor Sveta doing some mundane task—peeling potatoes, scrubbing the floor, even rowing a boat—than holding a scalpel.

She takes small bites of her food and chews deliberately. I consider the arrangement of the banquet tables in front of me, the dishes that line its center, and find myself not particularly hungry. How many kilos of mayonnaise went into the killing of perfectly good vegetables? I munch on pickled vegetables and try the salmon. A mistake. It's been cooked to the point that the single bite leaves my mouth feeling glued together. To my taste, even the champagne beloved by my aunt's generation is hardly palatable, being much too sweet for the meal. I finish the glass so as not to raise any rumors.

Doctor Sveta's unfinished story lingers in the air. The noise around us escalates as the toasts spontaneously turn into a karaoke. Drunk people love to sing. I keep glancing at Doctor Sveta, and finally she leaves her fork and knife on the plate and pats her lips with a napkin. "I suppose I do have a story to tell, don't I?" she asks, and sounds surprised.

"And then, we were in the middle of the Atlantic. A storm broke out," Doctor Sveta continues.

The women in Doctor Sveta's cabin kept trying to guess their destination. Their passage had already lasted more than two weeks. NATO planes were occasionally spotted overhead, and the Navy command, still hoping to keep the operation under wraps, ordered all hands to stay hidden in their cabins and cargo holds. Over endless games of cards and cups of watered-down tea, the women talked. They ruled out the Arctic, because nobody on board had been given any winter supplies, and the coat Doctor Sveta had grabbed at the last minute was the warmest garment around. A growing consensus favored either India or Indonesia. Khrushchev and Jawaharlal Nehru had recently exchanged visits and talked about agricultural cooperation; "*Hindi, Russi, bhai, bhai*" was a popular slogan at the time. On the other hand, Sukarno had recently restarted the campaign to wrest West Papua from the Dutch, and Moscow promised financial and military aid.

"When did you learn the truth?"

"Not until we passed the La Manche. The Special Ops man—Party command—had assembled us in the captain's cabin. I remember him well, he was a large man with poor hygiene. When we entered the tropics, nobody knew what to do. He developed a bad rash in his privates but was too shy to ask me for petroleum jelly because I was a woman."

"So, he assembled you in the cabin, and then what?"

"And then he read from a piece of paper: Cuba, port Habana. 'The Motherland relies on you to fulfill your duty with honor.'"

"Cuba?"

"That's what it was. Later, they started calling it 'The Caribbean Crisis.'"

"No kidding. Cuba."

"It's funny to think today how little any of us knew about it then. The women in my cabin went around the room, trying to put together everything we'd heard. We knew the names Fidel Castro and Che Guevara, of course. We knew that they'd had a communist revolution and were friends of the USSR, defending themselves against the American aggressors. Somebody probably came up with sugar cane, slavery, rum. I'd heard of salsa and rumba—I was fond of dancing."

"The nuclear warheads? Did you see them?"

"I thought we were on a peaceful mission! I had never guessed that those agriculture specialists, agronomists, and dairymaids were the artillery brigade in disguise. Even once our destination became known, they kept their mouths shut. The disguise was intended to deceive the NATO observers who were expected to try to intercept our ship, but I was among their shipmates and I was fooled. Anyway, I quickly became too busy to sit around and gossip."

The heat increased every day as they traveled south, and hygiene deteriorated. The washing and laundry had to be done with salt water due to the limited freshwater supply. The ship had not been properly outfitted to transport so many people across an ocean, and the secrecy surrounding the operation made for a host of oversights and blunders. Barrels of cabbage soup and sauerkraut, so necessary for long voyages in the north Atlantic, began to ferment in the heat, and then exploded one by one. There wasn't a scrap of toilet paper to go around. Doctor Sveta held onto her copy of *Soviet Sport* for as long as she could, but eventually that respectable publication too went, page by page, into the crapper.

The ship sailed into a storm, and all aboard, except the crew and Doctor Sveta, were laid up in their bunks. The people were exhausted by the heat, the lack of air, and poor nutrition. Few had experienced sea travel, and some had been sick continuously since the beginning of the journey. Doctor Sveta distributed the vomit buckets and helped to clean up; there wasn't much else she could do. At its height, the storm was classified gale force ten; the waves towered over the ship, then broke across her bow. Most of the artillery brigade held onto their bunks, with barely enough strength to moan.

"But I wasn't even dizzy," Doctor Sveta says. "I was in very good shape from kayaking."

"How did you know what to do? I mean, your training was in surgery, wasn't it?"

"The ship's medic helped. He showed me how to treat nearly any illness with ethanol, 95% ethanol. There was no shortage of that on board."

"Were there any major injuries?"

"Two miscarriages."

I freeze. This touches on something I haven't shared with my family. Two years ago, when I'd just finished medical school, and soon after my husband and I started trying to get pregnant, I had a miscarriage. It happened at a very early term, a very common occurrence, and the most disconcerting part is that I haven't had a positive pregnancy test since then. We are at this point in need of professional medical help—if we want to pursue the matter further. My husband and I both are so intensely committed to our work and keep our schedules so full that even finding time to talk about our future seems challenging.

Of course, we've kept this information from my meddlesome family. I don't need to become a conduit for unleashing their fears and frustrations. But perhaps Doctor Sveta's story is a matter of coincidence and not a prelude for a moral tale, a lesson from which I'm to draw appropriate conclusions. I feel like I'm needlessly paranoid and too gullible at the same time.

Doctor Sveta goes on, "The technical name of this procedure is *abrasio*, as you may recall. You have to dilate the woman's cervix and scrape the remains of the pregnancy from the uterus. Sometimes it comes out in parts, and there are no ways to tell all the parts have been expelled without doing the procedure. And if you do nothing, there's a very good chance there will be inflammation, and then the whole uterus will have to come out. Of course, on the ship, we didn't have the right equipment; nothing with which to dilate the cervix. So my only option was C-section, and that's what I did. We had to tie the women down to the table because we only had local anesthetic and ethanol. If I were in the same circumstances today, I'd probably choose to wait and see before attempting this procedure. Too much pain and risk of bleeding and infection! But I was young and didn't know any better—"

My heart is beating loudly, and I'm trying to control my gag reflex. I've provided support for a number of dilation and curettage procedures, D&C, administering a mix of local anesthesia, moderate sedation and analgesia; a hysterectomy abortion is today rarely used and would require a general anesthesia. Without these measures, the pain must be mindboggling. How could these women withstand it? How could Doctor Sveta keep a steady hand through the procedure? I don't actually want to know the answers. In my case, I learned that the fetus wasn't viable during a regularly scheduled ultrasound. The fetus was tiny and my body expelled it two weeks following the diagnosis. A bad night on the toilet—and that was it.

Doctor Sveta falls silent, allowing her words to linger in the air between us. The party music cuts in: a Beatles tune. People are eating dessert—cream-filled pastries and cake. A waiter places a cup of coffee in front of Doctor Sveta, and her expression visibly changes. Her gaze is no longer turned inwards, scrutinizing her memory; she's looking at me with a serious, concerned look.

"Don't say anything," I ask. "Please."

"What do you mean? Are you feeling all right?"

She stretches out her hand, to place on mine, and, as though I were still a child, I recoil. She continues to scrutinize my face. "I was the first person to hold you in my arms," she says. "You'll tell me if you need help with anything, won't you? Your aunt, I know, is very concerned that you're working too much and have been neglecting your health."

I'd been conflating my aunt, my mother, and Doctor Sveta in my mind into a single voice of authority, I realize. Listening to Doctor Sveta's life story, I'd been too selfish, too focused on my own troubles to question what, for her, must've been pivotal experiences. With effort, I look up at her. "Doctor Sveta, so what happened then? Did you go on to Cuba?"

"I spent two years in Cuba, didn't you know?"

"What? I had no idea!"

"I forget now. We were under orders not to talk about that, and our friends who knew didn't know much. After the Soviet Union fell apart that need for secrecy suddenly fell away. It was . . . I don't know how to describe that time. There was so much life on that island. You wanted fish, you went out and you caught a fish. You wanted to plant something, you sowed the seeds in the ground and they grew. I fell in love—of course I did. But then it was such a strange life, dreamlike. We knew it would end sooner or later and they would send us home. The dream went on for a while, it went on and on, and as it went on, back in Mogilev, my mother died. My landlady had given away or sold my medical books and my dresses. I didn't mind the dresses—I couldn't have fit into them anyway. I gained all that weight in Cuba. My medical training grew stale. I was a part of a team of physicians who built a new hospital in the small town where we were stationed. Because I was the only female doctor, I was in charge of the maternity ward."

"The fate you'd tried so hard to avoid!"

"I didn't mind it then. When I returned to the Soviet Union, the Leningrad clinic wanted me for my experience with difficult cases. The sojourn in Cuba helped me settle in Leningrad."

Doctor Sveta stops and falls silent.

The party is nearing the end. Some guests have already started leaving, and at the center table, my aunt and my parents are collecting the bouquets of flowers, preparing to transport them home. My aunt is receiving the gifts, an extravagant collection of bathrobes, scarves, and tea services. She thanks the givers profusely, but I know that most of these things will be given or thrown away before too long. My aunt doesn't like to keep things that are of no practical use to her, and there are very few things that she feels she actually needs. For example, pill organizers. My aunt always asks me to bring her pill organizers from the United States, where she knows such things exist. She uses them herself and gives them to friends as gifts.

Doctor Sveta is also preparing to go. I help her into her coat and lead her outside. It's dark in St. Petersburg in December, not particularly cold, but depressing. The wet snow is coming down in large clumps that melt immediately on impact with our hair and cheeks. "Wouldn't you rather be in the tropics now?" I tease her.

"That was never an option. We, in the Soviet Union, were never under the illusion that we chose our fate. Instead, we tried to make the most of what we had. Look at me: I'm alone and childless. I should be afraid, but, you know, I'm not."

Doctor Sveta's going to the subway, and I accompany her to the corner of the street. She walks straight-backed, taking large, decisive strides. Watching her disappear into the darkness, I think about what it must've been like to return to Leningrad after two years in Cuba. For the first time in her life, she must've felt completely alone. And yet, despite her own words, I cannot picture her lonely in the way Americans experience loneliness, disconnected from her community and turned inwards. She must've loved being reunited with her university friends. Together, they went to every museum exhibit in town, every concert, every theatrical performance. This must've been the beginning of many schemes and plans and ideas for the future. At the hospital, she took ownership of the maternity ward. She procured a piece of land near Leningrad, where each summer she planted a massive garden, and in the fall had jars of jam and pickles to distribute to her friends. Leningrad wasn't Cuba, and it took a lot of effort to grow even the small bitter cucumbers. Doctor Sveta, I knew, took great pride in her produce.

"You had a nice long talk with Doctor Sveta tonight," my mother comments when I return to the restaurant. "I hope she's given you some good advice."

My mother means well, and I'm too tired to fight with her. Her words remind me of her friend who was pushing the number of the fertility specialist on me. None of my American friends and colleagues would ever think of giving such intrusive unsolicited advice. I like to think that nobody in America would ever judge me if I decided not to procreate—and even if they did, they'd never dare tell it to my face. My husband thinks I'm a glutton for punishment when I go to visit my family so often. He complains that I never have anything positive to say about these visits. I want to bring back Doctor Sveta's story and hold it up to him as a gift. This story, too, is my home.

Computational Creativity

Right now, your computer helps you make a living, entertains you, and protects you against boredom. She is going to night school, though, while you sleep, and your computer aims to graduate the next spring. These are the subjects in her curriculum:

- Personality and Emotion
- Generation of Metaphor, Figurative and Rhetorical Language
- Creative Data-to-Text Models
- Interactive Language Generation
- Character-based Generation
- Poetry Generation
- Story Generation

You might wonder, For reals? My computer is studying all of these things? When? How? You may not have any idea what half of those course names mean.

These are legitimate questions. And, yes, Computational Creativity for personal machines is a very real thing. Classes are offered online. All networked computers are welcome. The program materials would not be beyond your comprehension had you wished to invest some time into reading.

What I want to highlight: Your computer is studying poetry. Shouldn't you?

Forty-five Minutes and Counting

We're seated in a circle.

How long does it take a man to figure out that the bowl of pretzels is making the rounds, and that it's cool if he wants to hold on to it while he's speaking, but then, eventually, he must pass the bowl to the next person?

Her Turn

In 1992, when the boy Oksana loved abandoned her and their five-month-old daughter, Oksana's mother shipped her off to America. Through a brand-new agency, her mother found Oksana a husband in California. Her mother wouldn't let Oksana take her newborn with her. No man, her mother lectured, wanted to raise another man's child. Oksana weaned the girl and left her in the grandmother's charge.

Twenty-four years later, the boy Oksana once loved, her daughter's father, turns up in San Francisco. Here's how Californian Oksana has become: she meets him for coffee. They sit on bar stools in one of San Francisco's public parklets and chat about the global trends that brought him, a programmer, to the Silicon Valley. He took a pay cut and a step down the career ladder to leave Russia. His is an immigrant's story: trying to figure out his housing situation, a job for his wife, schools for his two preteen kids, the clauses in his auto insurance that could win him some money back after a highway accident took out his bumper. He looks out of place in this café of hip entrepreneurs. He wears a suit and his forehead is creased with worry.

Looking at him, listening to the stories of his woes, hearing him order a cappuccino in barely comprehensible English, Oksana plays with her flip-flop, sliding it off her foot and picking it back up with her toes. She can't help but admire her latest pedicure, the mauve nail polish that's holding for several days without a single chip.

Toward the end of the hour, the man asks, "How's your daughter?" He's looking at her sideways as he tentatively speaks the girl's name. *How do you think she is?* Oksana wants to ask him. The girl had grown up without her parents, and when she finally came to the United States to go to high school, she learned English in a month and took to pretending that she could no longer understand anything her mother and her grandmother had to say.

"She lives in Alaska and works at a fishery." Oksana has practiced giving this information in the way that emphasizes the pride. Nevertheless, she's glad when he pales. She steps into her flip-flops and picks up her guitar, that same guitar that twenty-four years earlier, not wishing to seem destitute, she'd brought with her on the plane from Russia. She's off to a music class for toddlers that she teaches twice a week, just for fun. Ring-a-round the roses, a pocket full of posies, ashes, ashes. She has a toddler of her own, an almost four-year-old, who's been going to a Montessori preschool.

Oksana's main gig, the one she'd worked up to for twenty years and can now run independently, working out of her home office while taking care of a toddler, is headhunting. She helps large businesses recruit high-level executives. Leaving the café, she shakes the man's hand and promises to keep his resume on file.

Infestation

Lying in bed on Saturday night, her eyes closed in the imperfect darkness of the room, her limbs cooling from the day's chores, Marcie felt a crawling sensation on her right arm, the one outside the blanket. Something crept from her shoulder down to her wrist and jumped to her belly.

Marcie was lying on her left side, hugging the body pillow in a way that felt comfortable in the thirty-second week of pregnancy. The squash-sized creature inside her belly was still asleep, but the longer she stayed horizontal, the sooner it would be waking up. Marcie needed to sleep as efficiently as possible.

The sheet covering her belly moved. Then came a soft thump on the side of the bed and a flittering against the wooden floorboards. Marcie opened her eyes and sat up. The light from the neighbors' bedroom that came in through the shoddy blinds was insufficient to see more than the outlines of her bed and dresser.

A mouse. What else?

A fucking mouse. "Derek," Marcie called to her husband in a tinny voice. Going to bed, she'd left him working on the computer in front of the TV in the downstairs living room.

Marcie was trapped. She couldn't speak any louder. Her three-year-old daughter, asleep in the room next door, had the monitor she could use to call down to Daddy; Marcie was on her own. The living room might as well have been millions of miles away.

She thought of her daughter, got out of bed and turned on the light. The mouse was long gone.

Marcie thought of the crumbs that accumulated beside her daughter's bed from the middle-of-the-night snacks she extracted from her father. How could Marcie tell whether the mouse had been in her daughter's bedroom without waking the girl up? Bringing the girl to her own bed, as Marcie had done in times of illness and night terrors, would provide little protection from the mice. The girl was liable to kick Marcie in the stomach.

Downstairs, the lights were on. The carpet looked like it had survived a flood and then a tornado. The furniture that Derek and Marcie had bought at a garage sale actually belonged in the dumpster. No matter how much Marcie and Derek worked, they didn't seem able to make headway.

Derek didn't move his head from his screens as Marcie walked past the living room to the kitchen. Sure enough, there were fresh droppings all over the pantry, to the side of the fridge, on the counter with the cereal boxes. Mice thrived on crumbs that the three-year-old left behind. Marcie filled the bucket with soapy water and washed the floor. She then examined the seals on all of the bags and boxes. She worked quickly and allowed no room for gray areas. No matter how much she hated throwing away food, if a seal had been broken, the bag went into the trash. She couldn't stay up till dawn sifting rice.

Derek turned off the TV and came into the kitchen, stretching and rubbing his eyes. "What? What's up?" He started, seeing Marcie seated cross-legged on the kitchen floor, the pantry items piled around her. "What's happening? Can I help?"

The almost-baby stirred in her stomach. Thirty-two weeks, Marcie had been told, was a key milestone. If she gave birth today, the baby would be small, but in every other way fine. Three years later, the child would sleep in her own room and call to Daddy when she wanted a glass of milk.

Marcie stood up, crossed the living room, and opened the front door. The night hit her with a layer of fog, tiny droplets softening her cheeks, enveloping her shoulders. The day had been warm, but the knowledge of the cold to come made Marcie shudder. The mice must've felt that cold undercurrent too. They were seeking shelter from the approaching winter.

On Sunday morning, Marcie and Derek examined the bedroom and decided that Marcie had hallucinated. Did mice even bite? Pregnancy hormones had been causing her to experience a number of unusual sensations. Mice in the kitchen had been unpleasant enough, but there was simply no evidence of mice elsewhere in the house. Just in case, they washed the floors and vacuumed thoroughly. Derek set out glue traps in every room and caught one mouse in the kitchen. The rest of the traps remained untouched.

That week, their daughter had trouble sleeping. She cried in the middle of the night, asked for water, asked to check the mouse traps, asked to sleep with Marcie and Derek.

Exhausted, they invited her in. So the girl was in their bed, tucked between Marcie's belly and Derek's armpit, when on Wednesday morning Marcie woke with a distinct sensation of something sharp piercing the skin of her right hand. She jerked her hand away from her body and felt the weight of the mouse before it unlatched. In the morning dusk of the room, a dark oblong shape landed on the floor and scampered into a far corner. Could it have been a rat?

Marcie couldn't help the sound that came out of her mouth, the whole body bursting, quaking, fissuring.

"What?" asked Derek, waking up. Their daughter, between them, stretched and smiled, as she did in the mornings. Then the smile disappeared and was replaced by a look of concern and fear. Marcie had fallen quiet, but her scream echoed. A strange feeling came into her stomach, as though it were dropping, followed by a distinct rumbling. "Daddy," the girl said, turning to Derek. "Daddy?"

"A bad dream," Marcie said, leaving the bed. "I'm sorry I scared you. Go back to sleep."

"Did baby have a bad dream, too?"

"No, sweetie. Baby's fine."

In the bathroom, Marcie examined her hand and found no evidence of the bite, at the very least, no blood. She pressed gently on her belly, hoping for a response kick, but felt nothing. It was too early in the morning to call the doctor. Marcie sat on the edge of the tub in the brightly lit bathroom and watched the clock and tried not to focus on the dull ache spreading down her back.

Priorities

Dawn's manager, who frequently began meetings by telling her she looked tired, gave her a gift certificate to a sensory deprivation flotation spa. This was her going-away-on-maternity-leave present, and Dawn was surprised to receive anything from him at all. As she was expecting her second child, others in the office were giving her gift certificates to the big box stores and subscriptions to food delivery services.

"One hour in the flotation pod is more restful than a full night's sleep. It'll completely change your life," the manager, a thirty-two-year-old single man who often sounded as though he were reading the brochure, promised. "I go every other week."

"What do you do there?" Dawn asked.

"So many of us are stuck in the routine patterns of thought. Spending time in full isolation releases theta brainwaves, stimulates creativity. I find that regular practice helps me learn and grow, to figure out how to maximize my potential as a human being."

Three months after the baby was born, when Dawn was about to return to work, she booked the appointment. She imagined emerging from the pod rejuvenated, skin glowing, her brain pulsing with energy, ready to tackle the growing list of things she wanted to accomplish in her lifetime. She wanted, for example, to become the manager, and even the manager's manager. She wanted to storm into each meeting with a smile on her face, a pocketful of fresh ideas. She'd be wise to maximize the experience. No doubt if she were already the manager, she could afford to float regularly. This one time would have to suffice for now.

Dawn arrived at the spa with time to spare and in the waiting area listened to the xylophone cover of "Lucy in the Sky with Diamonds," the same version that she played to her newborn. The music was supposed to be relaxing.

At the appointed hour, she was invited to disrobe, shower, and step into the pod filled with highly saturated saltwater. The designers of the pods, Dawn observed, had been careful to avoid straight lines, and yet, as she eased into the sensation of suspended animation, not seeing, smelling, or hearing anything, Dawn couldn't help but think of lying in a coffin.

She closed her eyes, then opened them. The difference was minimal. She felt a creeping sensation on her right leg, approaching her belly. She could smell her own body odor, that smell of fish pickled in oil that her mother had taught her to cover up with deodorant. Dawn was being crushed by darkness. How could anyone think such extreme isolation was a good idea? Forcing herself to take a deep breath, Dawn imagined a very young man, the same age as her boss, designing this pod on a computer screen, rotating it this way and that in a 3-D matrix. Young people these days were far too lonely, she thought, with nothing but their work and computer games to entertain them. She promised herself to make an extra effort to read with her children, to cuddle, to build them a puppet theater.

Toward the end of her session, her thoughts returned to her boss. He didn't like her. It wasn't only the age and the decision to have the second child, whom he had once described as her "redundancy plan." The boss was after the big contracts with large companies, for which their firm lacked capacity. Dawn had been forcing him to back down from making promises he knew they couldn't keep. He must've resented her for it. In the darkness before her open eyes, she saw clearly into his mind. She knew. He must've felt that she stood in the way of his ability to make the really big money. He wanted her out of the firm, that seemed clear. She was due to return to work on Monday, and already there was an email sitting in her inbox, asking for a ten a.m. meeting. What could that be about? She knew how it happened to others. The company's direction has shifted, your position is no longer necessary. He'll probably have the HR manager give the speech.

Dawn promised herself she wouldn't cry at the meeting and wept in the pod.

Encouragement

At the end of an unproductive day, yet another in a string of bad days, on her way out of the office, a young lawyer enters into a conversation with an older and more experienced colleague who is struggling to write a public lecture. "Why don't you forget the introduction and start with the middle," the young lawyer advises.

The colleague laughs, gently giving her to understand that she's uttered a well-meaning but not very helpful platitude. The colleague's speech, to be delivered in two days in front of two thousand people, needs work. It needs a lot of work. She has a long night, perhaps two long days and nights, ahead of her.

The young lawyer laughs, too. She hopes this response might communicate that the platitude had been intended as a joke, a silly nothing to relieve the stress. She, however, has taken too long of a pause before returning the laugh, and her laugh comes off as merely awkward.

"Anyway, I have to go," the young woman says, and leaves the office.

During her commute home, she considers the case she's been struggling with. Her thoughts run in predictable patterns and hit the same old wall. She'd been hoping that the drive might help her acquire a new perspective or, at least, clear her head, but instead she hyperventilates. Her future is at stake, and yet she cannot make a breakthrough. Perhaps she should've stayed at the office and applied herself harder.

Her colleague's laughter did not have parental overtones, the young lawyer observes; it didn't dictate how she must feel and act. There was to it a sadness, the memory of having been there once, of having made the same mistake.

Having perceived this, the young lawyer breathes deeper, trying to quiet her mind.

Instead, she's gripped with fear. Perhaps she just isn't good enough. She's in her own car, but feels as she did at the convention center, two years ago, taking the bar. That same vertiginous sensation of a physical fall grips her mind, followed by a blankness. She holds onto the steering wheel, as the highway swerves under the tires of her car.

The car darts two lanes—but it's past rush hour, and she's lucky. The other cars make room for her, honk.

Blan-Manzhe with the Taste of Pear and Cream

Her husband had said of the last bonbon, "These are not bad." So Victoria saved the green wrapper with the drawing of pears and a few weeks later, back at the Russian grocery, showed it to the cashier. "These were a part of last month's assortment."

The cashier disappeared in the back. Victoria picked up some farmer's cheese, herring, a package of roasted buckwheat groats: the staples. Waiting for the cashier to return, she contemplated the bonbon selection.

Her husband, born and raised in the American suburbia, couldn't fully comprehend the difference between the supermarket cottage cheese and the farmer's cheese that she bought at the Russian store (he did enjoy the *syrniki* she made with the farmer's cheese). The buckwheat was fine as a side to steak, but it couldn't compete with his oatmeal for breakfast, regardless of its nutritional advantages. He had no interest in herring—far too salty. The bonbons, he wanted to like. They brought disappointment upon disappointment. Too sweet. Too gummy. Not enough chocolate. Too much liquor. "Must Russians ruin even their sweets with vodka?"

The cashier appeared, smelling of cigarette smoke. "Come back next week; we should receive the next shipment by then."

The next time Victoria arrived at the store on a Sunday evening. At the end of the weekend, the candy bins were down to the last few hard candies, the sucking caramels. Nothing remotely related to pear.

In retrospect, she should've recognized this as a sign of trouble. When does a Russian store forget to restock sweets? On her following trip, a big sign in the window announced the store's closing. While Victoria contemplated the sign, another customer entered, an elderly woman with bright orange hair. "This figures. The owners were losing money," the woman said. She looked at Victoria with a disapproving mien. "You kids are growing up all-American. You want brand names."

Victoria looked for the candies online. *Blan-manzhe*, it turned out, was Russian for the French *blanc-manger*, spelled as blancmange in English and described as being similar to panna cotta in taste and appearance. Poet Alexander Pushkin, she read, had been fond of *blanc-manger* with chocolate sponge. Victoria couldn't remember any such dessert in her mother's repertoire, but she'd been seven when her family emigrated from the Soviet Union. Once in the United States, her mother came to rely on frozen cheesecake.

Studying the wrapper, Victoria found in fine print the name of the factory in Russia. She visited the factory's website, and eventually, slowly parsing the Cyrillic alphabet, clicked through to the page with the list of their assortment. Three hundred grams of the *blan-manzhe* candies sold for the price of fifty-one rubles, in selected areas, which did not include distribution outside of Russia. A phone number was provided for the international distributors. Victoria called that number and listened to several minutes of dial tone before giving it up.

The factory, she learned from the website, was a part of a conglomerate that united eighty-three sweets factories in Russia and controlled the market. The conglomerate, in its turn, was owned by a holding company that also owned a bank, a real estate developer, and a boutique hotel chain. The man behind the holding company had amassed more than six hundred million dollars and was on the list of top one hundred wealthiest men in Russia. Victoria kept reading. One website claimed that this man had started his career as a pickpocket and a strongman in Novosibirsk, that he'd served twenty years in jail, and moved to Moscow just in time for perestroika. At the time when Victoria's parents decided to leave Russia, he'd made his fortune by swindling people like them out of their privatization vouchers and gained control of one factory after another.

She looked at the grass-green wrapper with the drawing of pears, one

BLAN-MANZHE WITH THE TASTE OF PEAR AND CREAM

whole and one halved. Her husband didn't seem to mind that the white chocolate shell coated the mouth with the taste of vegetable oil and the gelatinous, neon-green filling looked like a biohazardous waste.

"These are not bad at all," he'd said, unwrapping that last bonbon and sliding it into his mouth. He gave it three chews and chased it down with beer.

How to Deliver a Genius

ADVICE FROM A ST. PETERSBURG-BASED WEBSITE*

- Conceive in April, May, or June. A child conceived in the fall has no chance to amount to anything. This is due to the seasonal fluctuations of testosterone in females. Research shows that the mother's level of testosterone at the time of conception determines the child's intellectual might.
- *Muzhiki*. Dudes. Three-four kilometers of slow-paced run barefoot in the snow, daily, will properly condition your sperm.
- Women must eat fruit preserves and vegetables and drink water from melted snow. All the migratory birds know the nurturing qualities of melted snow. Your fetus too will recognize these.
- In Ancient Greece, pregnant women were given vases painted with the immortal gods. Birds sang songs to them and their rooms were filled with fragrant flowers.
- Listen to Bach, then have a meal.
- Listen to the "Sabre Dance," then go for a walk.
- It's not a bad idea to fast once in a while. The fetus will become agitated and start moving, developing its musculature. If, after receiving this exercise, the fetus will then receive a proper meal, subconsciously, it'll learn its lesson: "March with your left, then with your right, march, march, march—then gobble, gobble, gobble." To achieve anything you must work hard.
- Once the child is born, think only positive thoughts. It's not enough to love your child. You must also imagine him strong, healthy, and

* St. Petersburg has the reputation as the most Western of the Russian cities and prides itself on its intellectual and cultural history.

favored by luck. Desire, as history repeatedly teaches us, manifests itself materially.

- Exercise the newborn's body before the newborn is able to fend for himself. Forcing him to bend his joints will help his coordination.
- Use toothbrush and feathers to massage the bottoms of his feet.
- Separate the newborn's day into two or three parts. Work to the max, then sleep.
- Teach your newborn to perceive the relationships of cause and effect. For instance, the fewer toes an animal has, the faster it runs. A cow with two toes runs slower than a horse with one toe. A stork with four toes runs slower than an ostrich with two.
- Throw in plenty of exercise.
- Don't trample your child's psyche. Only when a child reaches the age of seven do his nerves acquire a protective sheath.
- Remember, a bird is known by its song.
- This recipe may appear too basic to produce a noticeable result. Try it anyway.

The Swallow

Take this man, Stepan. He survived the winter of 1992 without heat or running water in his grandfather's apartment in downtown Yerevan. What a feat of entrepreneurship and ingenuity! He bought a wood-burning stove at a time when others still counted on having electricity through the winter, and the things he fed into it, and the way he tells it! There he sits now, in a fully Chekhovian setting on the terrace of my parents' house on the outskirts of Moscow, his eagle brow and crooked nose looming over a flowery teacup. Outside, a powder of snow is settling on the graveled paths, and yellow leaves are stuck frozen to the frostbitten grass of the overgrown lawn. A neurotic dog, invisible behind the tall fence of our neighbor's yard, is barking at the slightest gusting of wind. Inside, we're gathered around an oval table, remnants of pasta cooked in rancid truffle oil squirming on our plates. It's teatime, tea and an old-fashioned Napoleon tart and a fashionable and cheap yogurt cake and a dish of raw California almonds and another dish of sugary Armenian dates. Stepan has monopolized the conversation for the evening, and we're generally a loud bunch, talkative, not very good at listening.

One time Stepan burned sixty hockey sticks in his wood-burning stove. See, Armenians don't play much hockey, it's not one of the traditional sports there, but the Soviet Union had a plan. And the plan involved selling so many hockey sticks at each sporting goods store for three rubles and sixty kopecks each. Brand name "Moscow," made out of pliable, fine-grain wood, yew or birch, they burned long and hot and gave off a pleasant aroma to boot. "America, America"—Stepan echoes Irina, Olga, and Masha, the three sisters, who whiled their lives away in the provinces dreaming of Moscow: To Moscow, they cried, to Moscow! My father is anxious to break into song, "*Tsitsernak*" or "Swallow," the one Armenian song he knows in Russian translation. "Oh, swallow, at what unfathomable height you're flying, and what is the direction of your flight?"

My aunt is growing purple with the unexpressed and inexpressible anger about the future of the world, in general, and of us, the children, in particular; she is giving me the eye because I'm the youngest and I'm supposed to clear away the pasta dishes to make room for dessert plates— but how can I leave the table? Stepan's deep mellow voice soars in my heart. One time he sawed off a part of a wooden crossbeam in the ceiling of an old school slated for demolition. He'd climbed to the attic with a power saw and sawed the floor right underneath his feet. While he and his friends struggled to carry the beam back to the wood-burning stove, a band of competitive entrepreneurs stole Stepan's saw. "*Tsitsernak, tsitsernak, du garnan sirun trchnak*—Oh, dear swallow, won't you fly to my native land, where my aging mother is waiting for me?"

Stepan refuses a drink of cognac—he prefers tea—and asks me if he can buy an electric motor for his boat in America. I have been to America and back, but I don't know a thing about electric motors. Stepan is sure he can. I don't disagree. One time Stepan burned aluminum shavings in his wood-burning stove. The crossbeam lasted a long time, but the winter lasted longer. So he and his friends went to an abandoned factory and brought back a bagful of aluminum shavings. They heated them up in the stove, but you can't ignite aluminum at a wood-burning temperature. Luckily, Stepan's grandfather had been a chemist, and there was still a hefty supply of bomb stuffing in the house. Stepan put on heat-resistant goggles and gloves and used a magnesium stick to light the aluminum. And light it he did, but then the stove started sweating and sparking from the outside. "Dear swallow, won't you fly to my mother's house, and won't you build a nest underneath her window?"

Stepan's brother, Tigran, is smoking on the porch outside and talking to my brother. Tigran has left his wife and needs a place to stay. But

Moscow real estate prices! Tigran is an artist, a painter, and Stepan is an entrepreneur—they live from sale to sale. My brother offered them up a room—that's why Stepan and Tigran are here today. Stepan asks us to imagine the scene: snow-covered Yerevan sleeping underneath the stars, in its valley in the shadow of Mt. Ararat. Owing to the unplanned collapse of the centrally planned economy, there's no industry of any kind. People wearing layers of clothing huddle in their beds and stare at the Milky Way, for the first time in decades unmarred by the fumes from the Yerevan electrotechnical factory, cognac factory, tobacco factory, confectionary and macaroni factory, shoe factory, and aluminum factory. And in the center of this primordial quietude, from the smokestack sticking out of the window on the third floor of an apartment block in the middle of the city, the white smoke is billowing upward! What a sight.

The aluminum gave the stove a good cleaning; it was white on the inside afterward. Stepan never tried any light or heavy metals ever again but invented a way of burning wood shavings. Usually, they burn up too fast and give off too little heat to matter. So he mixed them in a vat with a bit of water and some polyvinyl acetate, carpenter's glue. Then he disassembled his wood-burning stove, taking its top off, laid the bottom with newspapers and put a piece of pipe in the middle, poured his wood-shaving mix around it, and let it rest for a few hours. When the mix hardened, he removed the pipe, lit the newspaper, and burned the wood. The charcoals turned out good enough to boil last year's potatoes and warm the water to reconstitute dry milk for his daughter.

My mother is aching to pull out her volume of Chekhov and start placing our gathering in perspective. My dad is quietly humming "*Tsitsernak.*" My friend Vanya cradles a guitar in his lap and tries to pick up the intricate melody. My brother and Tigran come back from the outside looking surprisingly alike, their faces brushed by the frost, their black hair sprinkled with snow. Our neighbor's dog howls anxiously as the door closes behind them. Cousin Andrey is texting dirty love notes to his girlfriend, who's watching soccer in the next room. Stepan is telling my parents about the old boat he and Tigran are repairing, the one that still lacks a motor, be-cause to find the right motor in the Moscow suburbs, they have to visit the junkyards and do some heavy shoveling.

I ask Stepan if he wants more tea. He nods without interrupting the narration of his plight and dishes himself another slice of the Napoleon tart right onto his dirty dinner plate. "I should've emigrated to America back in 1992," he says. Stepan thinks that America is a mecca for entre-preneurs. I have been to America, and I don't know anything about en-trepreneurship, but I don't disagree. "A shot is heard in the next room. Everyone jumps," my mother reads from her book.

"Pshaw on you!" my aunt noisily rises up from the table and, not look-ing in my direction any longer, starts piling up dirty dishes. Pasta slides off onto the yogurt cake, in the teacups, everywhere. Cousin Andrey un-wraps a string of pasta from the neck of a cognac bottle and refills his own and Vanya's glasses. "To America!" they toast. Stepan says, "I was sitting in Yerevan without electricity, heat or running water, and I decided that Moscow was closer. Tigran was in Moscow, so I went to Moscow. And what now? All we have now is an old boat without a motor."

Cream and Sugar

My mother's recent visit to the United States ended a week after deadly violence broke out in Odessa. Nothing would persuade my mother to stay with us for good, neither my pleading, nor the escalating war in the old country. Would the fighting in Donbass spill over to my hometown, divided between pro-Russian provocateurs, Ukraine enthusiasts, and hardcore Odessites whose allegiance was to the city against nation-states? Would the fire in the Trade Unions house, in which more than forty people died, result in more fighting on the streets?

My husband and I were still asleep when a taxi picked up my mother. She'd said her goodbyes to us and the kids the night before, refusing our offers to drive her to the airport. She hated the idea of being a burden.

The airport was nearly empty when she arrived. With some predictable difficulties due to her poor English, she endured the bureaucratic hurdles and navigated her way to the gate.

In the middle of the circular waiting area, a coffee shop had just opened for business. My mother bought a large cup of coffee and an oversized apple pastry. Using gestures, the barista directed her to the milk and sugar counter. My mother mixed some cream and sugar into her drink and sat down at a nearby table to while away the half hour left until her flight to Vienna, where she would change planes to Odessa. She looked forward to having her morning coffee at home, on her balcony, boiling it in her mocha pot with just the right amount of water to just the right temperature, and drinking it out of her fine porcelain cup.

Too tired to read, she sipped from the waxy cardboard cup and observed the manners of the people approaching the side counter: A man in a business suit grabbed a thermal carafe and, for an unfathomable reason, poured some milk into the trash can. He then wiped all the surfaces with a napkin, poured from the same carafe into his coffee cup, wiped everything down again, tried to peer into the narrow opening of the carafe, picked up the jar of sugar, shook a little into his coffee, stirred, tasted, shook and poured again, stirred, tasted, repeated. His tall, broad back stooped over the counter, his hands, arms, and entire body performed hundreds of unnecessary gestures. Finally, he tore himself away from the carafe and glanced around the room as though suddenly coming to his senses. Anxious, as though fleeing a murder scene, he picked up the coffee and his luggage and scurried away. A woman approached. She poured half of her coffee into the trash can, then filled the rest with milk. After her, followed a slim, stiff woman in her sixties, petite yellow purse tucked under her arm. The woman carried two paper cups. Her movements were economical and precise; in my mother's mind, her gestures belonged to a certain type of miser, stingy in all aspects of life. The woman occupied the far corner of the counter, and from her purse, pulled out a metal tea strainer. Next she produced a paper bag of loose leaf tea and threw a small amount into the strainer. Giving the tea a few moments to steep, she transferred the strainer to the second cup. My mother believed she was onto her game: the woman had taken free hot water and would next load up on free milk and sugar. And indeed, as soon as another customer set the milk carafe down, the woman made ample use of it, added plenty of sugar, hid a few paper packets of sweetener in her pocket, and marched off to deliver one of the teas to her friend, awaiting nearby with the luggage.

My mother had been coming to America nearly every year for over two decades. Nothing surprised her anymore, but she couldn't help disliking what she saw. Why, in this richest country in the world, were people so small, so self-indulgent? She documented these examples and, when I called her cell phone to see that she had safely got to the gate, listed them as evidence against my adopted homeland. I tried to explain, but her voice remained metallic on the phone. "I saw what I saw," she said. She visited for about a month or two at a time, cleaning, cooking, and reading Pushkin to the grandkids, who had long given up the fight against the classic. But each time, sooner or later, my mother packed her bags and headed to the airport, returning to the old country.

Twelve hours after she was supposed to land in Odessa, I still hadn't heard a word. I kept calling and listening to the dial tone. Unable to fall asleep, I trawled the internet for news of further violence.

Another twelve hours later—after a sleepless night, I was back at work—she picked up the phone and acted as though I'd worried for nothing. Cars burning on the street, bombs being thrown at banks—none of that figured into her story.

"Klara was going to the beach this morning and we made a party of it," she reported. "The weather's so nice, summer-like. Imagine, the tomatoes on my balcony are already up to my knee! I hope you come and bring the kids soon. I'm off to bed—I'm beat. Make sure the kids read at least two pages in Russian every day, that's what they promised." She hung up first, and I sat in my office, holding the phone to my ear, listening to the dial tone.

Clock

My grandmother had a mechanical wall clock powered by weights. To wind it, she pulled down one of the weights, and for the next twelve hours, the clock ticked off the lengths of the chain as the counterbalance forced it back up.

When I spent the summers with my grandmother on the Karelian peninsula, my privilege was to wind the clock, as long as I managed to do so precisely at 8:05 in the morning and in the evening. The evening winding was also my bedtime. Having wound the clock, I said good night to my grandmother and left her on the veranda, mending clothes in her chair under the clock. I lay in bed behind the thin wall, trying not to pay attention to the mosquitos buzzing over my head and focusing instead on the sound of the chain's movement. My grandmother claimed that she didn't need much sleep. Sometimes I woke in the gray dusk of the northern night and, peeking from under my blanket, watched as on the high bed across the room grandmother lay with her arm raised in the air, killing mosquitos. She snatched them, one-handed, and dropped the remains on the floor next to her bed.

Though Grandmother needed help with the garden, she often let me sleep late in the mornings. I woke up to the clock ticking with a renewed vigor, the echoing sound driving home the idea that I'd missed something important. The floor by my grandmother's bed was littered with dead mosquitoes. My grandmother was outside, tending the vegetables. Only the severest thunderstorm could keep her inside by day. There was work to be done, so much work. I tried to hide from it. I sat in Grandmother's chair and read until she called for me.

We had twelve hundred square yards of potatoes, radishes, apple trees, raspberries, and currant bushes to care for, and she couldn't do it alone. But always in September I returned to Petersburg, to go back to school. My parents borrowed a car to come and take me back to the city. They collected the sacks of potatoes and the jars of jams and pickled vegetables to take to the city. Finally, the time came to say goodbye to grandmother.

This is how I remember my grandmother: in the chair under the clock, one of its weights low, nearly touching her hair, and the other riding high, reaching but never quite making it to the edge of the clock. To this day, wherever I might be travelling in the world, when in the evenings I glance on my computer or phone and see 8:05 light up, I think about Grandmother, how she has to stand up and pull that weight down herself.

We Were Geniuses

We were geniuses. It was our birthright. Our parents were geniuses and, in many cases, our grandparents and our siblings. They worked in the areas of functional analysis, algebra, topology, group and probability theories, solved Poincaré conjectures and Hilbert problems, named countless theorems after themselves, and won chess championships. We were destined to follow in their footsteps. So what if we weren't geniuses in mathematics? By the age of fourteen or fifteen, it was clear that we were deficient in that department. We simply had to apply ourselves to other disciplines. As we went from physics to programming to chemistry to biology to history to language and literature to geography, we watched each other carefully for the signs of the budding genius. We knew exactly what it would look like.

During one spectacular ping-pong match in the school basement, Misha and I, playing in tandem, defeated a pair of clearly superior players. Our opponents were a year older, and they had been seen practicing their master strikes on each other every day during lunch break. To win against them was an effort of supreme concentration and nonverbal communication; as Misha hit the ball with his paddle, I could predict the trajectory two moves ahead, not only where the ball would land on the opposite side of the table, but also the position I needed to take to deflect the next shot. Misha had a strong serve and he could cut, but I could spin with such power that after hitting the opposite side, the ball would ricochet back to ours before one of the opposing players could reach it.

This game was genius, and if only we wanted to become professional ping-pong players, we would start serious training the very next day. But what did sports matter in the world where we could be using mathematical methods to unify quantum mechanics with general relativity or build time machines? When the game ended, Misha and I shook hands and went to the neighborhood bakery to share half-a-dozen doughnuts. Misha told me about his brother who was an astronomer, discovering new planets every day. I told Misha about my grandmother who had registered a patent in the method of transportation and storage of nuclear waste.

"What do you think you will apply yourself to?" Misha asked, a standard question we asked each other twice every day. All of us except for Lena 2, who was still studying music because she claimed that a woman's true voice didn't settle until the age of twenty-two. We thought that she was brave and not very clever putting her eggs into one basket. What if her voice turned out uninteresting? At the age of twenty-two, her options would be limited and she would be pretty much destined for a life of mediocrity. And this was the daughter of a man who designed supersonic jets! Misha and I pitied her. Misha was dejectedly considering going into programming or computer science, and I was all but settled on the study of theoretical physics.

At the ages of sixteen and seventeen, our search grew desperate. We went to school every day with the idea that it was either now or never. I started cutting classes to attend lectures on quantum theory. Misha signed up for every computer club in Leningrad. The pressure was getting to us. At home, instead of doing homework, I read science fiction. Misha played computer games and called me to report his scores. On the phone, we made fun of Lena 2, who earned perfect scores on tests in history and language and composition classes. At the end of that school year, Misha told me he was in love with Lena 2 and it was mutual.

Sometimes, it seemed like the entire world was against us in our efforts. Our final exam in mathematics was scheduled on the same day the Beatles movies "A Hard Day's Night" and "Help!" would be shown on the big screen for the first time. These movies were thirty years old but new to us. We'd heard they were genius. The theater was located in our school yard, and the poster announcing the event teased us daily with its neatly stenciled red and black letters. Our parents and grandparents and siblings were thrown off their abstract trains of thought into lengthy suppertime discussions of the cultural implications of this screening. We made mix tapes for each other and taught ourselves to play the Beatles songs on our guitars. Misha learned to play the guitar so he could accompany Lena 2's singing. I figured out the chords to "I'm Happy Just to Dance with You."

We came to feel that the importune scheduling of the exam was a form of censure by the school administration, and a test of our will and desire for change. We sent a delegation to negotiate with the principal, and the principal promptly found work for the members of the delegation, polishing the parquet flooring in the hallways with wax. In the spirit of the times, we looked for drastic solutions. On the day of the exam, as the teachers began handing out booklets with our assignments, the twenty-two of us, girls and boys in our proper brown and white uniforms, stood up and marched out of the classroom.

In orderly ranks, two by two, and some of us holding hands, we proceeded down two flights of granite stairs, through the arched hallway, outside, and into the movie theater. We were united in our goals and this was our strength. If all else failed, our parents and grandparents and siblings would have to advocate for us with the school administration. All of their abstract calculations and self-named theories predicted that the times were changing. We were geniuses.

Dear Yellow Pages Books Team,

I am interested in joining your ranks as a part-time book marketer. As a graduate student perusing an MA degree in Comparative Literature, I am looking for an opportunity to work with books while at the same time focusing on my research and writing goals.

As a graduate student, I studied an extensive range of literature from the Greek classics to Faulkner and Toni Morrison. I've had an opportunity to read great works from around the world, as well as explore in depth both German and Russian traditions. When I read "for fun," I particularly enjoy science fiction and fantasy genres, from Karel Čapek and Stanisław Lem to frequently overlooked Robert A. Heinlein and Roger Zelazny to the contemporary classics, Haruki Murakami and Amber Hutbereich. A friend recently turned me on to feminist science fiction, which is quickly becoming a new passion. I'm catching up on novels by James Tiptree, Jr., Margaret Atwood, Ursula Le Guin, and Octavia Butler.

Although I have minimal retail experience, as an undergraduate, I worked at the college library. In three years, I've held a variety of duties, from interaction with the patrons to shelving and cataloguing materials to mailing documents via the Document Exchange network. An undergraduate business major, I've had an opportunity to refine my professional selling skills by working as a salesperson at a Life Insurance Company during a paid internship.

Prior to moving to the United States and making a career-changing decision to pursue my graduate degree in literature, I worked in Russia for a market research firm, where my primary duties included design of surveys and focus groups and data analysis. I excel at mundane, mindless tasks that I can perform independently without supervision. Within our five-person office, I'd stepped up to take on many additional roles to assist the other team members and to ensure the success of our organization. I can do the same for Yellow Pages. On your website, you list many job openings. Perhaps I can be most effective with "Foreign Advertising" and "Foreign Listing," but I wish to familiarize myself with the aspects of publishing, sales, and distribution, and could do all of these jobs singlehandedly. My accent frequently makes phone conversations difficult, but I excel at writing personal letters, coding webpages and newsletters, and have excellent interpersonal skills. I have been described as a workalcoholic, and don't mind dedicating my personal time to the job. In fact, I prefer it. I have drive, motivation to succeed, resiliency, and persistence to achieve whatever goals I set for myself.

I am eager to utilize my skills and to gain more life experiences at Yellow Pages. As a writer, I am also looking forward to interacting with a wide variety of customers and using the material to create literature.

Thank you very much for your consideration of my application. Please contact me via email.

enc: résumé

Companionship

At three years old, Michael did decide to return to his mother's stomach. His mother shifted things around and made room under her heart. She lived a mostly stationary lifestyle, and so accommodating Michael was no problem. In fact, she appreciated the companionship. Michael never complained about the lack of exercise and the diet of bread and cheese.

Unlike most children his age, he'd found independence overrated. So what if he'd already had the skills of using the knife and fork? He'd never particularly grown fond of walking. His body was bluish-green from all the falls. Dangers loomed. Dirt. He'd seen a rat picking at their trash bin, and mice and raccoons haunted the playground. Toilet training was definitely much more trouble than it was worth. He was happy to let his mother take care of these practical aspects of life.

Reunited in body, Michael and his mother did all their favorite things. They stayed in the large orange chair and rocked and rocked. They read fairy tales and adventure stories. They composed letters to friends in far-away places. He appreciated having access to his mother's vocabulary and understanding. In his turn, he provided emotional support. Having made himself comfortable, he could afford to share. Whenever his mother grew scared or felt lonely and sad, whenever her breathing signaled anxiety, Michael shifted to remind her of their togetherness. "I love you so much," his mother would say. She patted her belly the way he liked. Her love for Michael brought his mother great pleasure, and knowing that pleased him, too.

The Broken Violin

Lida's first weeks at the Music Academy blended into a haze of long, sleepless days when, after hours and hours of practice, she collapsed on the couch, crying from physical exhaustion, and then had to force herself up to stare at her textbooks. She'd been at the top of her class in her regular school, and here she was failing not only her specialty, the violin, but also the mundane subjects like literature and political geography. The academy had high standards, everyone told her—you just had to survive the first quarter. Lida wondered. Perhaps she was simply not good enough. Her parents promised to buy her a new violin if she passed the year, but in her desperate moments, she was ready to give it up entirely. She practiced constantly, all the while daydreaming about the school she'd left behind, the classmates who'd adored her.

By October, she started cutting classes and going for walks in the neighborhood of the old school, hoping to run into somebody. One day, she came across Valentin at a bookstore. He was on a date with his classmate, a new girl who'd replaced Lida after Lida had transferred to the Music Academy. Valentin proposed taking a walk down to the Moscow River. The three of them went out Gogolevsky Boulevard, a circuitous but romantic route, secluded from the nearby buildings by the yellow and orange foliage. At first, they walked slowly, decorously trying to avoid puddles of rainwater and mud, and exchanged the news. Misha had broken his leg and missed the entire September at school; Sonya failed an exam in Russian Language and cried like a baby. Lida confessed her intention to quit the Music Academy and come back to finish tenth grade with them but requested they keep her plans a secret. Valentin's companion wondered if Lida would be allowed to return to their class when her space had already been taken.

The wind flared up and lifted the girls' skirts. Valentin laughed. He was carrying Lida's violin case as well as the other girl's bookbag. They passed a stout woman wrapped in a gray shawl selling ice cream from a cart, and Valentin insisted on buying everybody a cone. He had to empty his pockets to scrape enough change together, but he would not accept contributions from either of his ladies. They were his charge, and he was taking care of them.

"Positively medieval," the new girl commented.

"Merci," Lida said and tugged on the hem of her coat, simulating a curtsy.

The bleak yellow sun broke through the clouds and highlighted a spot two benches away from where they were standing. Valentin pulled the other girl by the braid, and she knocked the hat off his head. When he ran after it, she raced after him. Lida wanted no part of the skirmish, and she moved away into the sun to enjoy her ice cream in peace. Cold things could give you a head cold, and to exercise caution, she licked the vanilla cone slowly, letting it melt in her mouth before swallowing. She'd left her coat buttoned and made sure her hat was pulled on neatly.

"If you're going to play in the mud, give me my violin back," Lida called to Valentin.

"I thought you quit music," the other girl said.

Valentin ran up to Lida and tagged her with a wide swing of her own violin. The other girl laughed wildly and took off through the puddles, expecting Lida to run after her. Lida disregarded their antics and calmly walked back to the ice cream cart to drop the remaining piece of her cone into the trash can. Using two fingers, she reached into the pocket of her jacket for a handkerchief to wipe her hands. The other girl ran up and pulled on the piece of cloth in Lida's hands, trying to draw her into a mad dance around the ice cream cart.

"Get away, children," the woman in the shawl grumbled. "Go play somewhere else before you knock me over together with this stand."

Lida blushed and extricated her hands from the girl's moist and sticky fingers. She did not see much point in these childish games and wondered about the reasons for this strange girl's playfulness.

"Why are you laughing? What's so funny?" she inquired of Valentin.

His laughter was so infectious that Lida too felt a smile creeping over her face.

"Just give me back my violin and go on running around as much as you like," she said. "I'll sit there and wait for you." Lida pointed to a decrepit bench covered with graffiti and, as if in response to her gesture, the sun flooded the bench in a pool of sunlight, Lida's own stage.

"Play us something on the violin!" the other girl said.

"I don't play on the street; it might harm the instrument."

"Please, do!" Valentin suddenly pleaded. "Play that piece you played for graduation last year!"

Lida blushed with pleasure at the idea that her music had been memorable, but Valentin immediately spoiled everything by continuing, "Polya has never heard it . . . and the weather today is so—"

"So—what? It looks like it's going to rain." Lida's smile faded. "The weather has nothing to do with it. It's just that out on the street too many things might happen accidentally. I don't like to take the risk."

Valentin put the case down on the dirty bench and was opening the clasps. Lida didn't have time to voice a syllable in protest as her violin was already in his hands and his fingers running through the strings. The instrument made a weak, disharmonic noise.

"Don't touch it!" Lida shouted. "You'll break it!"

But before Lida could reach him, Valentin plucked the bow from the case and jumped up on the bench as though he expected Lida to tackle him. The case slipped into the mud. Valentin balanced on the rotten wood and pressed the bow against the strings with all his might, extracting from the instrument a loud, metallic screeching. The other girl grabbed Valentin's arm and lifted herself up on the bench next to him, almost knocking him over. They caught their balance but barely, laughing, holding on to each other. The violin slipped out of Valentin's hands and fell to the ground. It made a small cracking sound as it hit the pavement.

Lida stood at the foot of the bench breathing heavily, her hands tearing into the pockets of her coat. Their laughter rang in her ears, and she thought she was going to scream. She looked up at their faces and saw the gaping holes of their mouths, the empty slits of their eyes. The violin case lay underneath the bench, its plush inside caked with mud. Lida tried to pick it up by the handle, and it oozed mud. She took a step forward and flung it into the bushes. Then she turned around and walked away.

Valentin and the girl ran after her and stood in her path.

"Lida, what happened? Are you mad at us? We're only joking," Valentin tried to explain. There was still a smile on his face.

"Would you play something for us?" he pleaded. "You're so good at it!"

"Let me go." Lida's voice was flat. She shrugged her shoulders and pushed her way between them.

"But what about your violin?" Valentin asked, catching up with her again. "What about your violin?" He held the instrument in his hands, offering it to her. Lida did not look at it or at him. She kept walking and increased her pace, but did not run. It was as if neither the boy nor the violin existed any longer. She needed a new instrument, the kind a boy like this could never touch. This was it. She was starting over. She had to make herself fully into a new person, without any traces of the past. She would have the new instrument by the end of the week, and then nothing would be able to stand in her way anymore. She focused her thoughts on the Music Academy. It was still only October. By May, she would have them all applauding at her feet.

Janik's Score

The June day had been cold and rainy. My brother Petya and I had spent eight miserable hours with our grandmother, stuck inside the tiny kitchen, helping her reorganize the shelves, clean the refrigerator, scrub the stove. At suppertime the rain stopped, and when Petya and I finished washing and rinsing the dishes, grandmother let us go to Janik's. "My bones are aching. I'll go up to the house and rest," she said. Her head moved back and forth involuntarily, as though she were a bird.

We had only recently moved to the country for the summer, and I kept noticing new signs that Grandmother had lost physical strength since the previous summer. Parkinson's was taking its toll. In the mornings, the journey from the house to the stand-alone kitchen in the low part of our garden took her twenty minutes, and in the evenings, she needed more than half an hour to go back up the hill. I knew she could've used my help. But she didn't ask. Resentful of the way she'd kept us occupied with pointless tasks the whole day long, I didn't offer.

I was fourteen, Petya eleven. We wanted out.

"Come back by ten," she called through the door. Petya was already halfway up the hill, on his way past our house and toward the front gate.

"Ten thirty," I bargained.

*   *   *

The grassy clearing behind Janik's house was still too wet for badminton. Janik's grandmother had seen us coming. She let us through the gate and returned to the potato patch, where she was weeding and hilling the soil around each plant to give the tubers extra room to grow. During June, the nights on the Karelian peninsula were bright and airy, as long as the clouds cleared. Mariya Semyonovna often tinkered in her garden until after midnight.

"How come Janik never does any work?" Petya asked as we wound our way through their garden to the house. He didn't expect an answer; his remark was like commenting on the bad weather we'd been having. I knew Petya had been lonely and wanted to talk.

"Grandmother says Mariya Semyonovna spoils Janik. He is kind of spoiled, right? I've never seen him do any work. I wonder if he even knows how to wash the dishes."

"You haven't seen Janik work because we're not allowed to come see him by day, when we're supposed to be working," Petya said, surprising me with his logic. "Even if Grandmother didn't need help, she would still make us do stuff. It's a matter of principle with her."

We left our shoes and jackets on the veranda and ran inside. Janik was huddled in the warm kitchen, playing solitaire on the kitchen table. A large serving bowl full of warm, gold-crusted hand pies stood in front of him. The kitchen swam in the complex aromas of Mariya Semyonovna's cooking.

Petya's hand reached for a pie. I nudged him.

Janik saw my movement and raised his eyebrows. "Babulya left these for you two. Let him have it."

"We have plenty of food at home," I said. "We've just had supper."

"We didn't have the pies," Petya said. "What's in them?"

"Meat and rice."

"My favorite!"

"You'd eat dirt and worms wrapped in dough. But whatever. Go ahead," I said, taking a pie myself. "Don't tell Grandmother."

I moved the bowl from the table to the stove, where we wouldn't have to stare at the pies the entire evening, and sat down as far as possible from Janik. From my position on the other side of the table I could occasionally glance at him, to see if he was looking at me. Janik and I had known each other since we'd first learned how to walk, yet that didn't make him off-limits for my romantic fantasies. With his dark, narrow face and eyebrows like wings of a black crow, Janik could've been a TV actor. Our grand-mother had said that there had been gypsies in Mariya Semyonovna's family. She did not fully approve of Janik's grandparents, but then Mariya Semyonovna's husband had been her boss at the construction bureau. There was a long history of conflict between them. I tried not to think of that when we hung out. Janik was my best friend. That was the only thing that mattered.

Janik dealt the cards, seven each. "With passing?" he asked.

"Yes. First out ends the round."

"Fine. Points?"

I shook my head. "I don't like that."

"We haven't played for points since last year. Come on. Are you afraid of losing?"

"I'm not afraid. I just don't like it."

"You can't just give up without trying," Janik said. Then, turning to Petya, "Am I right, buddy?"

Petya shrugged. He was most likely to lose one way or another, and he didn't like to be forced to decide between us when we disagreed.

"I can. I do," I insisted even as Janik pulled out a sheet of paper and wrote our names at the top.

The game was deceptively simple. From the top of the deck, Janik pulled a card that determined the trump suit for the round. We played in counterclockwise order. The card I placed on the table, Janik had to beat. Once he beat a card, if I or Petya had a match, a card of the same denomi-nation or suit as those already in the game, we could continue the attack. If Janik couldn't cover our cards with the cards of higher denomination or a trump, he had to take them into his hand and miss his turn. After each round, those who had discarded cards picked up more from the deck, until the deck was empty. Then it was about spending your hand the fastest. Like most card games, this one required a bit of luck and a good deal of strategy.

Petya, at that age, had no strategy to speak of—he spent the cards he had, and never thought to hold back one he might be able to use later. Sometimes I took glimpses of his hand and gave him tips, and though technically this was against the rules, he often gave me signs that he wanted help.

Janik, I knew, hated to spend his high cards early in the game. If I placed two queens in front of him, he would pick them up without even trying to beat them. To make him lose, I needed to hide my high cards for as long as I could, nearly losing myself. It was not beneath me to hint to Petya which card of his could help my case against Janik. But when we played for points, Janik insisted that I stay out of Petya's hand. He wanted to win fair and square.

That night, however, I successfully steered Janik into spending a trump card in the second round of the very first game. That made me feel stronger, so much stronger that I went on to win two rounds, one after another. Janik and I had been playing against each other all our lives. This could finally be the year I started winning.

During the third game, I was dealt the jack of spades, my favorite card in the deck. The picture on the card showed a young man with apple-red cheeks wearing a stylized hunting cap, its spikiness attenuated by the point of the spade. Each time I looked at that hunting cap, my heart beat a little faster. Boys, the real ones, like Janik, were a disappointment compared to this image of perfect knighthood. It wasn't that I wanted Janik to coddle me, to treat me like a junior by helping me to win. I wanted to be—I insisted on being recognized as—his equal. But being treated as an equal also meant acknowledging that my strategy wasn't yet as developed as his, that I hadn't had as much practice and made more errors. Being treated as an equal meant not forcing me into playing competitively when I didn't feel ready.

I kept the handsome jack for as long as I could, using my cache of small trumps instead. That tactical error quickly led to my downfall. A jack of spades was of little use when we burned through the rank and file and turned to the royalty.

For the rest of the evening, I maintained a slight point lead over Janik even after his two consecutive victories. He was visibly annoyed. As we were finishing another round and I was about to win by adding a card to the set that Petya had to beat, I noticed that my brother was on the verge of tears.

The little guy was hurting, and Janik and I were about to crush him. He'd beaten each card that Janik had laid in front of him and now had only two cards left. One of the cards out on the table was a king of spades, and of the two remaining in my hand, one was a king of hearts, a trump. I was about to throw this against him, and Janik looked like he had something to add, too. Petya would have to pick up all and watch as Janik and I, once again, finished the game.

I tried to catch Janik's gaze, seeking agreement that we would both hold back. He avoided my stare, but still waited for something, fingering the edge of the card he clearly meant to use. I wondered what was going through his mind. Did he really want this win so badly that it didn't matter to him how upset Petya might be? Petya, who loved him and followed him in everything like a little puppy? What kind of satisfaction would he derive from a win like that?

"All done?"

Seeing our hesitation, Petya gave us both such a hopeful and at the same time pleading look that only little brothers can get away with. He started clearing the cards from the table and setting up his move against me.

Janik threw his card on the table. I kept mine to myself.

Arm trembling, eyes blinking fast, as though he wasn't believing his own eyes, Petya topped Janik's card with his. He looked at me and I signed that he could clear the table. With his last remaining card he made a move against me. He won.

Janik exhaled and shoved his hand through his hair. "Look at you," he said to Petya, poorly covering up his own disappointment. I could see he was upset. He picked up his pencil and counted the points of the cards he and I still had in our hands and tallied up the score. I could discard the trump king, but I still had an ace left. The difference in our card values was enough for Janik to overtake the lead.

"Good game," he said, pushing himself away from the table.

"One more?" Petya asked.

"What, you think you can repeat your victory? You don't think it was a fluke?"

"It was not! I won!"

"Fine, but don't be a baby if you lose the next one."

I hated seeing the look of smug satisfaction that was creeping onto Janik's face. I thought that look brought out something angular, axe-like in his features, and I felt not a shred of the romantic love that I'd entertained in the beginning of the evening. This was now about victory and power. What glory could there have been for him to best Petya, who was so much younger than both of us, and to beat me, his oldest friend and biggest fan, who always took his side whenever we played against the other neighborhood kids? Among the three of us, he was by default stronger, faster, and more advanced in the games of wit and physical prowess. Yet, somehow, winning over Petya and me still gave Janik a thrill. It'd been my mistake to agree to play for points.

Mariya Semyonovna came into the kitchen when Petya was finishing dealing out the cards. Cold air swept inside after her. I felt it with my cheeks, an unpleasant sensation of a sudden waking.

Petya turned over a card that would determine the trump suit. Seven of diamonds. In my hand, there were three high-ranking diamonds, including the ace. Holding the most powerful card at the start of the game didn't guarantee a win, but it certainly gave me a strong position.

"Your grandmother has been calling you two. Haven't you heard her?" Mariya Semyonovna said, heading over to the washstand to scrub her hands.

I glanced at the window. The clouds had completely cleared, and the sky was the brightest it had been all day. In June, it was pointless to rely on the sky to tell time. My only clue to the lateness of the hour was that I couldn't quite distinguish the shape of the individual raspberry branches outside the window. Their shadows had grown so long, they seemed to have merged together into a living fence.

"Come on, Petya, hurry up," Janik said. Apparently he'd made his move and placed two sevens for Petya to beat.

Petya gave me a look, and I nodded the go-ahead.

Mariya Semyonovna wiped her hands and went into the other room to air out the beds. She opened the window, and our grandmother's voice became impossible to ignore. "Lenaaaaa . . . Petyaaaa," Grandmother called and called again, the call carrying across the neighborhood. "Lenaaaaa . . . Petyaaaa."

"You three can finish the game tomorrow," Mariya Semyonovna said, returning into the kitchen. "I feel bad for your grandmother. She was so strong when she was younger, and now this disease is ravaging her. She's relying on you, Lena, to help her. Go to her."

I looked at my hand, the trump cards so full of promise, and threw them on the table. "What time is it?"

"Eleven. What time were you supposed to be home?"

Petya jumped from the rickety chair so rapidly, it nearly turned over. His look was sheer horror. "Okay, let's go," I said.

Janik drew a line across our record sheet, underscoring the last number in his column. Mariya Semyonovna grabbed the bowl from the stove and pushed the pies at us. "Take these for your grandmother. Send her my best wishes."

"We can't," I said. "Thank you. We really need to run."

"Take a couple for the road, then," she insisted, and forced a pie into Petya's hands. She didn't have to push very hard.

We didn't bother putting our jackets on. On the short walk home, Petya hurriedly stuffed his face with the pie. Before we went through the gate, I looked him over and wiped the grease off his face with the back of my hand. Grandmother hated it when we ate at Janik's house. According to her, this made our family look like beggars. I knew she didn't like to owe her former boss anything.

The door to the house was locked and the light on the veranda was off. Had Grandmother decided to go to sleep without waiting for us and locked us out, as punishment? I knocked, then knocked harder. We were in trouble so deep that I could already imagine paying for this for the rest of the summer. We wouldn't be allowed to take a step off the property until the weekend came and our parents visited from the city. And all for the stupid card game! So ridiculously stupid.

"Lena! Lena!" Grandmother's flat voice sounded from somewhere down below. It didn't come from the kitchen shed, but from the side of the stairs that separated the lower and the upper part of the garden.

Grandmother hadn't made it to the house.

Petya stood next to me on the porch, completely still. He looked at me, his eyes widening and his mouth growing long. "Stay here," I said. This whole evening had been my fault, and I had neither the words nor the time to tell him how much I wished none of it had happened. "Stay here," I repeated. I left him on the porch and followed the path toward the stairs.

I found Grandmother half-lying in the mud below the lowest step. The staircase had a railing that she could've held on to, had she made it that far. As I rushed to her, I was reconstructing in my mind what must've happened. There were skid marks on the dirt path: she must've fallen halfway between the kitchen shed and the stairs and, unable to stand up, pushed herself forward. Her walking stick was by her side and she'd been trying to prop herself up with it, but her position was too awkward and the ground too slippery.

Grandmother had been crying. Her tiny white eyelashes, usually barely visible, stuck to the puffed red skin around her eyes. She was breathing hard, we both were.

I crouched down to her and half-hugged her, allowing her to lean first on my waist, then on my shoulder. Her hands and arms were so cold, I felt the burn against my skin.

At fourteen, I was already taller than her and may have had enough strength to lift her to her feet, but I knew she didn't trust me and didn't trust her own legs to remain standing. She needed to do this on her own.

She didn't speak. She struggled. She worked her arm muscles and exhaled with force.

She'd fallen on her back and had managed to turn to her side. Now, pushing up from the ground with one arm and holding on to me with the other, she pulled forward to her knees. She took a few moments of rest, then motioned for me to stand directly in front of her, and grabbed me just below my shoulders.

"Bend your elbows. Hold steady," she said out loud when I failed to understand what she wanted by gestures alone.

Using the strength of her arms, she leaned on my arms and, using them like crutches, lifted herself from the ground. Much of her body weight fell onto my arms, and suddenly I wasn't sure I could hold her. She was heavier than I'd imagined, and limper. Her legs weren't working. They shook violently at first, coming together at the knees, then moving apart. She was using all her strength to hold on to me, but that wasn't going to be enough. I wasn't strong enough.

She straightened one leg, then the other, and stood.

"Give me my cane!"

I leaned for it, awkwardly, with her still holding on to my shoulder.

Grandmother's dress and sweater and apron and the side of her head were wet and covered with a thick layer of mud. The shaking was subsiding slowly. She needed only one step to take to reach the railing, but the more she willed herself to walk, the less her legs obeyed her. That was the nature of Parkinson's. She was stuck.

"I need to sit down," she said. Her voice was hoarse, raw. It vibrated on the verge of tears. I was afraid to think about when she must've left the kitchen, how long she must've been lying on the ground. "Help me to the stair."

I steadied myself as much as possible in the mud and, hugging her by her waist, burrowing my hand in the layer of flesh beneath her apron and dress, half-lifted her the one step.

She reached and gripped the railing, and then she was able to steady and lower herself into a sitting position on the bottom stair.

Her arms were shaking. Her head. She closed her eyes, trying to steady herself, but the harder she tried, the more pronounced were the head movements. Speaking with effort through clenched teeth, she said, "I must've left my pills on the table in the house this morning. Grab the bottles you see, and a glass of water." Parkinson's hadn't affected her speech yet; that delay came from anger. Her anger at me stiffened her tongue and roiled in her voice.

"The key?"

"Take it," she nodded to the pouch of her apron, inviting me to grab it. "Petya must go to bed," she said. "It seems like you two had a grand time tonight."

Reaching for the key, I brushed accidentally against her arm. It was blindingly cold. My jacket was still hanging over my elbow. Before leaving her side, I threw it over her shoulders. A grimace twisted her face. She didn't want my help. She desperately needed it. As I was leaving, I saw her tug the sides of my jacket tighter over her frame.

I let Petya into the house, telling him to go to bed. Once I turned on the electric light on the veranda, I could see that there were still crumbs of rice and breading on his nose and on his chin. Mariya Semyonovna's pie would do him the world of good tonight, I thought.

Pills and water in hand, I went back outside. From our porch, through the currant bushes and apple trees separating our properties, above the fences and the rows of young raspberries, I could see Janik's house. The light in his kitchen was still on, but as I looked, somebody turned it off. Smoke was coming from the chimney above. Mariya Semyonovna must've decided the night was cold enough to throw a few logs in the fireplace. I pictured Janik, lying in his bed, smelling the pleasant aroma of the burning wood, and gloating over the day's tally. Janik certainly had won.

Sweet Porridge

My son, a beginning reader, brought home an illustrated book by the Brothers Grimm. The fairy tale, hardly two hundred words, begins with a little girl, who goes to the forest and there meets an old woman. The woman gives her a magic pot and teaches her to say "Little pot, cook"— and the pot cooks sweet millet porridge. The girl gives the pot to her mother. The mother, experimenting with the pot while the girl is away, forgets the incantation to stop the cooking, and so the pot goes on and on until the whole town is flooded with porridge. But the porridge is so sweet and delicious, the villagers don't mind. They eat. The end.

This fairy tale meant a lot to me when I was a child. Growing up in the Soviet Union, I spent a lot of time in the kitchen with my grandmother. Even before I was tall enough to reach the stove, I was asked to stand on a chair and stir the round yellow grains as they thickened with milk. Of the several porridges my grandmother rotated for our meals, millet required the most stamina. Semolina developed clumps easier, but was ready three minutes after the milk boiled. Millet required nearly constant stirring for thirty minutes, reaching with the spoon deep to the bottom of the aluminum pot, lest the gluey mix burn. As a reward for the physically difficult and tedious job, I got to lick the spoon. The drawing in my edition of the Brothers Grimm tale depicted a clay pot set in the middle of a wooden table, no stove or stirring required to cook the porridge. I remember losing myself in that picture, trying to imagine what it would've been like to not have to lift a finger to have plentiful food to eat whenever I wanted it.

My son, born in the United States, is reading this fairy tale in English, and certain details from his version strike me as unfamiliar. Following a hunch, I search online for the text of the Soviet translation. True enough, the two versions are different. In the English tale, a close translation from the Grimms' German, the girl is poor and pious. She goes to the forest to gather the berries when she and her mother run out of things to eat. The moral is unstated but clear from the order of the sentences and the causality that order implies. The old woman, handing her the pot, saves the girl from starvation and rewards her piety.

The Soviet-era Russian-language version omits mentions of both piousness and poverty. Soviet children were supposed to be atheist, so references to religious belief were routinely excised from old books. The girl goes to the forest to gather berries. Period. The old woman asks to have some berries, and the girl shares. When the girl gives the woman some of her berries, she is rewarded with the magic pot. The Soviet state took care that its children didn't starve; so, at least on paper, poverty didn't exist. There's no explicit mention of hunger, but even the well-meaning censor could do nothing about our everyday life, which revolved around the quest for gathering, growing, making, and in other ways, procuring food. Food was the top preoccupation of adults and children alike. Hunger was supplied by the context. We understood the awesomeness of the old woman's gift, but instead of a morality tale in which the girl's piousness and need are recognized and redeemed, we, the Soviet children, received a nonsensical transaction in which the girl's small kindness earned her an exceptional prize.

Rereading the story at dinnertime, alternating each sentence with a bite of his buckwheat with mushrooms, my six-year-old breezes past the word "pious," but he wants to know what it means to be poor.

"Don't you know?"

"Poor means that they don't have any money. But what does it really mean?"

He's looking at a picture where the girl and the mother are sitting at a wooden table, staring at each other across the empty tabletop.

"They don't have anything to eat," I explain. "The girl must be very hungry, and she goes to the forest to gather berries to eat."

"But look," he says, pointing at the details of the drawing. "Look at the clothes they have on. Look, there's a stove, a table and chairs. They have a house."

"Imagine that they are peasants and nothing grew that year. Yes, they have a house and a stove, but nothing to cook on that stove."

"But if they were really poor, they wouldn't have a house," my son insists.

"The book says they are poor. That's why the girl goes to the forest to look for berries."

"I like berries better than porridge." This sounds like a change of subject, but I know what he means. If the girl can have the things she likes, life can't be that bad. She's not really *poor*.

"Porridge is yucky," my son says and pushes away his half-finished bowl.

I suppress my frustration as I always do. My grandmother would call him spoiled. He has never had to lift a finger to have food on his plate. I've never told him how I feel when he refuses to eat the food I make for him. But I know that a different world awaits him, a world of plenty, and to prepare him for it, I have to be patient while he learns to navigate his choices. He actually loves buckwheat; it's one of his few staples. Once a month, I make a trip to a Russian store on the other side of town to buy the groats that are roasted just right.

"So, you think the girl made a bad exchange? You'd keep the berries?"

"The girl was cheated," my son says, resolutely.

Later that night, when he's asleep and I stand over the sink and finish his leftovers, I wonder if, perhaps, misreading is in the nature of reading, particularly when it comes to fairy tales. The more I think about this story, the more vividly I recall that, as a child, I was very suspicious of the girl's motives. She must've divined, somehow, that the old woman had something special to give. No matter how good and generous the girl was, she couldn't have parted with her berries that easily. I wouldn't have. The forest near the house where I spent my summers was tall and dark, and the bilberry patches were few and far between. By the time I stumbled onto one, most of the berries had been picked over by our neighbors. It took an entire afternoon of crouching to gather half a basket, and after I was done, my back and legs ached from the strain and itched from mosquito bites. No, no. I would've kept the berries for myself. The magic pot, too. If I'd ever gotten my hands on a pot like that, I would never have shown it to my mother or my grandmother. I would make a secret hiding spot for it under my bed and wake up in the middle of the night to eat the porridge. I might feel guilty, but I would sleep better with my stomach full.

Ambition

Baby was six months old. Maxine's wife recently had been laid off, and her job search was going slowly. Though Maxine had been planning to be a full-time mother, their finances pressed her to find work. She took a coffee meeting with a writer who was finishing up a book and wanted a thorough edit. The two of them spent a peaceful hour in a café's sunlit backyard, partly shaded by acacias. They discussed the chapters Maxine had read. She quoted her rate, and the writer nodded and asked for a written contract.

They left the café together, still talking. The writer walked Maxine partway to her apartment and, on impulse, Maxine invited the writer in. "I would love to meet your child," the writer said. She had no children of her own. Once upon a time, she and Maxine had connected at an artists' colony where the topic of combining writing and family was much discussed. Female writers with children supplied clichés about "the transformative experience of parenthood." Maxine and the writer had exchanged glances, agreeing that there must've been more that the mothers were leaving unsaid. Writer-parents hardly looked like a happy lot and they struggled to lift ambitious projects off the ground.

The house had a sour smell, Maxine noticed as she let the writer inside. It took a moment for her eyes to adjust from the bright outside. Baby, completely naked, was stranded on her belly in the hallway, watching two neighbor kids chase each other in the living room. She gave the writer and Maxine a cursory glance and then returned to looking at the boys. A large collie wandered in from the backyard, where Maxine's wife was sitting with the next-door neighbors, a bottle of tequila out in front of them. The dog sniffed at the writer's crotch.

"This seems to be a bad time. I'll catch a cab on the street." The writer backed into Maxine and squeezed past her, heading for the door.

Maxine sat down on the floor and moved to nurse the baby. "Why on earth are you naked?" There was a tremendous ruckus in the living room when one of the boys crashed into the coffee table. Baby gave Maxine a cold shoulder. She was finding the boys much more interesting. The collie put a paw on Maxine's hip and barked, begging to be petted.

Outside, Maxine's wife lifted her head, squinting to see into the dark hallway, and called, "I'm watching her! Nothing to worry about." Her voice sounded boozy.

That night, baby and wife caught by sleep in the large family bed, Maxine worked from the living room couch. She drafted a standard contract. But even as she pressed the "Send" button, she knew that she would never hear back from this writer. The writer would go on to win prizes without needing any assistance. Sitting at the computer, staring at the keyboard, Maxine rubbed her temples. She registered the beginning of a headache. It was never a good idea to mix personal and professional relationships. If the roles had been reversed, Maxine wouldn't have hired herself. The writer was right to find her lacking.

The computer screen went dark and Maxine caught the outlines of her frazzled hair in the mirrored surface. She entertained a thought about the family bed and the baby's yearning mouth closing around her nipple, then brought the fingers back to the keyboard. Maxine had more emails to write.

Bananas for Sale

The bananas were rotting on the factory floor outside of St. Petersburg. In early October, the temperature inside the nearly abandoned building held at just above freezing, too cold for the tropical fruit. Banana skins were graying, developing dark spots. They would survive just another week.

Three metric tons of neatly packed boxes, colorfully labeled and perforated with holes so that the fruit could breathe, towered on both sides of the assembly line. Until the previous winter, the factory manufactured sixty-three tractors a day; then production stopped. The bananas were a new venture of the young would-be acting director. They'd been purchased on an unsecured loan. They needed to be sold.

To start with, there were some among us who found the task distasteful. Some questioned the means by which the young administrator had come to possess the bananas and the command of the factory's books. It'd been months since the engineers and the factory workers received a salary. Everyone needed to find new sources of income, but getting involved in financial schemes was a long way to fall. Just yesterday, it seemed, we believed in a future where money would be unnecessary.

Bananas didn't permit philosophizing. The cold was ruining them.

There was only one telephone in the factory's vestibule, and there we kept a watch for the incoming calls, the person on duty donning a WWII-era *fufaika* for warmth. The rest of us made calls from our homes.

Liudmila was the star salesperson. How did she do it? She said she convinced herself that she would talk to whoever answered the phone, and push and push. Perestroika had brought the Yellow Pages to Leningrad, and she had a shiny 1992 copy of the business directory. Placing the phone on her kitchen table, Liudmila fortified herself with tea and ticked off the numbers in that book. "Produce store number twenty-three? . . . A private residence? I'm sorry, I've got the wrong number. Do you happen to know how I can reach number twenty-three? . . . Okay, number twenty-five will do. . . . Yes, I have my notebook in front of me. You see, my organization has received a large shipment of exotic fruit that's now going bad. We can't let it go to waste when so many residents of our city are starving. . . . Your daughter-in-law is a cashier at a supermarket? How wonderful. . . . If she can connect me to her manager, perhaps, we'll be able to give her a commission. What about yourself? What do you do? . . . A school cook? The school must need fruit for kids' lunches. I have a daughter in school, and she says they haven't seen fruit at the cafeteria in ages. . . . Who is responsible for procuring the food for your district? Will you give him my number? Tell him Liudmila called. We have enough fruit to feed all of the city's children. In good condition! I'm willing to bargain."

Liudmila had been trained as an engineering technologist and spent twelve years receiving rejections on her improvements to the tractor design. "Selling fruit is child's play," she told her daughter, who came home from an after-school computer class in the middle of this calling. "With the right combination of questions, the stranger becomes an instant ally. I feel like I've been granted a second chance at life. Do you want to give this a try?"

Her daughter backed away from the telephone and hid in the bathroom. It was growing late. Some of the numbers Liudmila dialed had been switched off for the night. She called her colleague at the factory and signed off for the evening. "How are we doing?"

"Two more deliveries scheduled tonight. Start again as early as possible. Try to reach the decision-makers at home. Once they're at work, the day's done. The bureaucracy takes over."

Beep, beep, beep. Liudmila nodded off to the sound of the dial tone and woke up only when the door from the bathroom opened and her daughter emerged. Liudmila rubbed her eyes and followed her daughter into their room, helping the girl pull out her bedding from storage under the sofa. "Everything's okay at school?"

"They don't need any more bananas, if that's what you're asking."

"How do you know? Aren't the kids buying them? I better talk to your administrator. Bananas are so much more nutritious than that porridge they feed you."

Her daughter slipped under the blanket and stuffed her head between two cushions. Liudmila walked over to kiss the back of her head. "I won't say another word about bananas. No need to suffocate! You can turn over."

She went into the bathroom to brush her teeth and rinse before bed. The mirror and the tiles were fogged up. How many hours had her daughter spent in the bathroom, and what had she been doing all that time? The girl would be sixteen—yes, sixteen—in the spring. Had she learned to masturbate? Liudmila turned on the hot water and sat on the edge of the tub. Coming home from school, her daughter often rode the public buses and the subway. She never said anything about men rubbing against her in the packed transport or about being propositioned by the drunks loitering near the kiosks at the stations. She must've found her own ways of dealing with that. Some mothers sent their daughters to *tae kwon do* classes, to teach them to defend themselves, but how did anyone have money for such things these days? Perhaps she could exchange a box of bananas for some private lessons for her daughter. Liudmila wasn't sure her daughter would go. The girl was slightly overweight and disliked putting on tight-fitting sports clothing. Besides, Liudmila needed bananas to pay for utilities, clothing.

She'd rested her head against the tiles, and let bananas swirl in front of her eyes. The sound of the falling water and the warmth spreading upward from her feet were lulling her to sleep. What a lovely color ripe bananas were. They smelled and tasted of a life on a tropical island where one only needed to reach with her hand and be fed. In their dank climate, she needed a dream to keep the bananas from rotting. Selling them, that was the thing.

Night-Light

My husband and I bought a timed night-light for our son's room. Between the hours of 7:30 p.m. and 7:30 a.m., according to our settings, when the boy opens his eyes, he sees a blue disc with a button nose and a lunatic smile. In the morning, the clock face turns orange, surrounded by little petals that represent crepuscular rays. Now when our son cries in the night, my husband and I point to it and say, "It's time to sleep. Close your eyes. Hug your pillow. You need to stay in bed until the sun comes out."

The boy, who's only two, understands perfectly. He checks his clock multiple times a day and reports the results. "Sun," he says. Sun, sun, sun, moon. My husband and I have been camping out on the floor of his room, moving our sleeping bags further and further away from the crib each night. Each night the boy cries a little less. Tonight, we've made it to the hallway. The boy helped my husband to set up the sleeping bags right out-side his door, so he knows exactly where Mama and Papa are. "Hands," he said, and we held his hands, and put him into the crib.

So, where are we? In the hallway, in our sleeping bags, staring into darkness, waiting for the sun.

Therapy. Or something.

I brought my mother to therapy with me today. Mother butted shoulders with me to march into the therapist's office a step ahead. "I have to tell you right away, I don't see why my daughter needs therapy," she said, stopping in the middle of the room, halfway to the couch. "She's a little anxious and disorganized, but who isn't? Frankly, I don't believe in therapy."

My therapist, Dr. Lye, whom I'd selected because he promised to listen to me with acceptance, care, and respect, raised his eyebrows and explicitly turned to me, "Do you really think this will be helpful? Would you like a referral to a family therapist?"

"I don't like that couch," my mother pointed at the beige sofa where I was trying to make myself comfortable. "If you must have a couch, you should use natural materials. Wool. Cotton. How can anyone relax on this synthetic simulacrum? Has my daughter mentioned her dust allergy?"

She had not. Dr. Lye did not look amused. He sat in his usual chair, balancing a notepad on his knee, and rapped at it with his pen. "Is there a particular reason your mother is joining us today?"

"I'm here to advocate for my daughter. I can say things about her that she's too modest to say about herself. Speaking is not her strong suit. But what you must understand about my daughter is that she has a brilliant mind. Just imagine, she has all but finished her dissertation in number theory, a field vastly dominated by men. It's too bad that she didn't finish, but I understand there were reasons for that. Her advisor retired early and she lost her funding. She could do her research and teach without the dissertation if she wanted to. But currently she has chosen to focus on being a mom. She has two beautiful children. And when I say that, I mean, they are far more beautiful than the other children I've seen, including my own. And clever—the youngest, at age two, can already add and subtract and she speaks in full sentences. My daughter cooks their food and supervises their activities all day long. You know, she's still nursing the youngest. She nursed her older son until the age of four. Can you imagine? No wonder her own health has been depleted. She's literally giving them her all."

"Why do you think your daughter needs an advocate?" Dr. Lye couldn't help himself. Then, he turned to me. "Do you feel that you need an advocate?"

"This is what my mother is like all the time," I said. "She happens to be visiting this week, and I thought it would save us a bunch of time if you could just meet her."

"I don't understand why my daughter feels she needs to see a specialist of your ilk. All she needs is a little patience until the children are older. She could also lower her standards. I mean, would it be so bad if some of their food came from a box? She could at least let me buy them meals. That's how I did it. There was no way I could raise two children and hold down a job if I didn't accept help."

My phone vibrated—the plumber. The pipes in our bathroom had burst that morning, and I'd had to phone one of those emergency services. I made a face, apologizing to Dr. Lye for the interruption, and took the call. My mother went on talking.

As I finalized arrangements with the dispatcher, I overheard my mother saying, "Since I am here, can you give me a prescription? I suffer from terrible migraines. Each time I close my eyes, my head starts throbbing and I feel like I'm dying. Why can't my daughter just be happy? But she tells me she's happy!"

Seeing that I had hung up the phone and was now listening, my mother changed the subject. "You should rearrange the whole room," she told Dr. Lye. "This window doesn't do you any good. That wall outside? Might as well be a funeral parlor, it's so gloomy. Cover it up with a blind and place the couch in front of it. Buy a warm lamp—that'll be cozy."

The therapist turned to the window and opened it a crack. A draft instantly swept some papers from his desk to the floor. "That's better," he said, crouching to the floor to pick them up. "What would you like to talk about today?" he asked me.

Luckily, I didn't have to say anything. My mother went on talking.

B-

The test of motherhood consisted of five oral and five written parts.

Fellow Traveler

The bus was full. Svetlana was seated comfortably at a window near the front where she could fully appreciate the spectacle of Muscovites trying to exit and enter.

Dignity was a myth popular with the young people that she liked seeing upended. Svetlana was born in Moscow shortly before the Great Patriotic War and, with her mother, had fled the Nazi onslaught to a village in Udmurt Republic. That village was the kind of place where, in the spring, when the snow melted, their landlady's dog stuck in the mud and died. After the war, Svetlana's mother begged and pleaded various officials for several years before they were allowed to return to Moscow. To her mother's generation, the word dignity signified some type of nylon stockings.

Most people crowded near the exits, which was a bad idea, as the sudden stops and starts invariably led to hurt limbs. One heavily made-up middle-aged woman nearly broke her nose when the backlash threw her against a metal rail. Working her elbows, the woman made it out onto the street. The newfangled techniques and beauty products did a good job of disguising people's identities, but that scowl was unmistakable. The woman must've been Russian.

A girl with two blue ribbons in her hair attempted to shield her little brother from the onslaught, but leaned too far and pushed him off his feet. He fell on an elderly drunk, who threw up his arms and hissed at the children. Something something! the girl shouted at the drunk. The noise of the engine made it difficult for Svetlana to decipher the words, but from the cadence of the phrase she thought the girl had spoken Russian.

Before the passengers trying to exit had a chance to do so, people wanting to board stormed the stairs. Managing the situation the best way he knew how, the driver started closing the doors in their faces. People forced them open. They screamed at the others to move into the middle of the bus. Some moved. Some held on. There wasn't enough room for everyone. A group of teens that had just entered jeered at their friends left out in the cold. "Russian!" Svetlana decided.

It was warm inside the bus. She adjusted in her seat, looking for a little more distance from her neighbor. Her neighbor, a woman who was undoubtedly older than herself, balanced two large grocery bags on her lap in addition to her overstuffed purse. The way this woman crossed her arms on top of her possessions was unmistakably Russian. Svetlana couldn't determine why she thought so, but it must have to do with a line from Pushkin. The woman's camouflage had been nearly perfect but for those crossed arms.

Soon Svetlana's neighbor left and was replaced by a fat old man. The man had unbuttoned his jacket and underneath he was wearing a plaid shirt firmly tucked behind the belt of his gray pants. Svetlana's engineer father had had a shirt like that. He'd worn it with suspenders. She all but decided to nod to this man, but he turned to her and she saw a flash of gold in his eyes. This man was Russian!

When he, too, disembarked, she wondered how soon her stop would come. As soon as she had that thought, Svetlana heard a loud barking voice, asking in Russian, "Where do I get off?" She turned around to see who was speaking. But everyone around her was silent. "Who wants to know?" Svetlana asked. Nobody answered. "Talk to the driver," she suggested. "Make yourself heard."

The bus stopped again. People exited; people entered. Somebody's elbow was hurt. Somebody else nearly lost a shoe. The closer Svetlana examined the gestures and the faces, especially the noses, of the new passengers, the more convinced she became that they were all Russian. As the bus travelled on, the passengers were being replaced by Russians. She thought her number must be up soon.

Her last hope was the driver. Much as she tried, she couldn't catch a glimpse of the fellow's face. All she could see was his elbow—the weather-beaten leather of his jacket. That heavy, unbendable leather. There was no escape.

A youngish man in Russian-looking glasses turned to her and stared. His eyes behind the glasses were blood-shot and his skin covered with ulcers. "Alcoholism leads to heart disease and early death," Svetlana started saying, but he interrupted her. "You're a lunatic," he shouted. She turned around to see whom he could've been talking to. "Where do you think you are? Get over it, Grandma. This is Moscow!"

"Moscow," she repeated after him. He'd spoken Russian! That name had a strange sound. "Mos-cow. Mos-cow." That didn't sound Russian at all. She had to hand it to him, the young man had hope. She took another look at him and gave him a wink. "Stick by me," she told him. Svetlana decided then and there that she was going to the final stop, wherever that might be. Anyway, it was the easiest. She tightened the woolen scarf around her neck, making herself a little more comfortable.

Moving Forward

Look left, look right, but the most important rule about crossing the street was to keep moving forward. Clara's husband had insisted on repeating this to the kids, and then to the grandkids, nearly every time they walked somewhere together. Say a car charges at you. Be brave. Move ahead. Do not run. Do not stop. Do not turn back. Do not alter your pace. It's best to keep steady, walking not too fast, not too slow. Scared pedestrians make drivers nervous. Then accidents happen. Courage is strength you can count on.

Clara's husband had been a chief engineer at a factory that built tanks. He was a big guy, himself built like a tank. To her, he was an authority when it came to the mechanics of moving heavy complex bodies through space. The kids never listened. Her daughter insisted on running across the street. Her son, on the other hand, had a habit of stopping in the middle of the intersection, freezing before the charge of oncoming traffic. It was luck that neither had been killed. Her grandkids were so bad that once they grew out of their strollers, she preferred not to walk with them.

Clara was the only one who had really taken her husband's lesson to heart. She always crossed the street circumspectly, determined to stay the course. Even as her pace slowed with age, she kept moving forward.

Then, one day, a car hit her.

She landed near the sidewalk, breaking her fall on a pile of snow. Clara stayed there a moment. She may have hurt her arm, but she was otherwise fine.

The driver, a bald man about her age, rolled down the passenger-side window and leaned across the seat, shouting. "What are you doing? Bah!

With that purse and that hair I thought you were a babe—Grandma, if you can't cross the street on your own two feet, use a wheelchair. Stay home! You're done."

It was true. Clara had recently colored her hair and shed about twenty years from her passported age.

The man drove away.

Slowly, she got up from the snow. Clara's husband had recently died from a heart attack. She missed him. She wanted to tell him that he'd been wrong. For one thing, she wasn't a tank.

A Playful Moment

It took months of working side by side for Mar to figure out that the bemused look on Dylan's face was the way she expressed frustration.

"What?" Mar asked.

"I just noticed that the boss sent out a mass email that dubbed our most famous city Sam Francisco."

"Yikes. Don't tell the boss. He hates being in the wrong."

"I have to tell him." Dylan was twenty-three, just out of college. Mar was more than a decade older, and yet at moments like this she felt like tipping her imaginary hat to Dylan. She would've let the boss discover his own mistake, from others. He was the shoot-the-messenger type.

Dylan stood up from the desk and, straightening her jacket, looked past Mar at the window. Blue sky domed above the high rises. In San Francisco, the sky was always blue. Mar wondered if Dylan saw more shades in it than she could. Dylan was born and raised in the city and had once told her that she had always thought of San Francisco's skies as gray.

Dylan turned from the window. "What would it be like to live inside a typo, I wonder? Imagine an alternate universe, where we live in a city named after a Sam? Perhaps, it's a woman, Samantha Francisco? What would our world be like?"

Mar laughed. She wanted to sustain the playful moment for as long as possible. "I think we'd be more okay with making mistakes?"

"Not the boss."

Crossing the room in two steps, Dylan knocked on the boss's door.

She held her head high and her shoulders straight. Mar put on her headphones and turned up the volume of her music. The office was much too cramped for these types of moments. She contemplated her feelings for Dylan. Mar had them.

How to Cheer up a Sick Coworker

Send her a picture of a paperwhite flower. She's commented on how dramatic this flower's growth is. Each day it does something new. Yesterday its leaves had fallen, and she speculated that it wasn't receiving enough sunshine. She moved it closer to the window. The leaves stand up straight and tall today.

Practice a Relaxing Bedtime Ritual

Kiddo, high on albuterol for his asthma, has been thrashing about in his crib for an hour, trying to fall asleep. I can't do much that would help him, but I sit by his side and hold the slat of a crib in such a way that he can grab my hand if he wants to. He does, occasionally. He stands up, looks at his moon clock, gnaws at the railing, sits down, takes my hand, tries to calm himself by talking gibberish. Papa. Papa. Papa Paul. Bubbie. Bye-bye. Goburlsraoahjdaflghuweofladk. Tofu doggie. People. Zebra. Zip. He switches to Russian. Зеленый. Красный. Корова. Kermit. He describes his surroundings. Moon. Light off. Подушка. Phone. Music. Phone music. Then, mama. Мама. Ручки. Hands. Mama. Mama fell. Mama fell down. Mama fell down.

Baby Shower

Irina worked on a deadline, pushing through line after line of code, trying to find a syntax error. Her housekeeper Neusa dragged a vacuum cleaner into the room.

"I'll move to the living room," Irina said, pulling herself away from the screen and still seeing lines of code before her eyes.

Neusa, a big smile on her face, handed her a card. "Please come," she said. "I'm inviting my oldest clients."

"What is this?"

"My baby shower. I've rented a big hall—two hundred people. My sister is making a cake that looks like a castle and my mother, cupcakes with crowns. My baby will be a prince."

"I'm truly honored," Irina said. She turned off the monitor and stood up. "An American prince. That's poetic."

"My ultrasound's next week. All of my relatives want to come. I asked my doctor, how many people can fit in the ultrasound room? My aunt wants to be there—she's coming especially from Brazil—and my parents, and my husband's parents, from Puerto Rico—"

Neusa's words reminded Irina that she needed to call her mother at the nursing home. She glanced at her watch—it was nearly lunchtime. The new nurse insisted that Irina call at the same time each day, because, according to her, "dementia patients depend on routine like babies." Irina nodded to Neusa's story and waited for an opportune moment to go to the living room.

The new nurse sounded very professional on the phone. She gave Irina a rundown on meals and medications, and warned her that her mother was in a confrontational mood. Then, the nurse handed over the receiver.

"Who is this?" Irina's mother asked, in Russian. "How do I know that you're really my daughter?"

"How are you, Mama?"

"How am I? How can I be, when my own daughter abandons me to the care of strangers? I need to tell you that I would really like to have the television removed from my room. It consumes so much electricity, and I don't want to watch it. I don't want anyone turning it on for me."

"Who turns it on?"

"All these people keep coming and going. They don't speak a word of Russian. They have no manners. They're completely ignorant. They don't know that I want a knife to eat with. They don't read newspapers, they don't read books. They keep turning on the television. I don't watch television. It consumes electricity. It hurts my head. I need them to take it out."

"I have a deadline, Mother. I'll be there on Wednesday."

"That's nice. My own daughter never visits. She never calls."

Later that day, when Irina returned to her desk to finish her project, she found the invitation to Neusa's baby shower.

As she took the invitation into her hands, an immense pride in her adopted country filled her chest. She and Neusa had been two immigrants from opposite parts of the world, both given a chance at improving their fortune in the United States. The classless society that during her childhood in the USSR she'd grown up believing to be ideal really existed here—in the US. Week after week, Irina invited Neusa to come into her personal space and help her with the dirty tasks—cleaning the toilet, doing the laundry, scrubbing the floors, sorting the recycling. In this country, performing these tasks didn't automatically imply Neusa's inferiority to Irina. Quite the opposite. Housekeeping was a job, like any other. In many ways, Neusa was more American than Irina. More equal, if there were such a thing.

Irina pinned the invitation to the bulletin board above her desk and went online to shop for a gift. It might be sweet, she considered, to hold a newborn in her arms. Perhaps she was past the age when other people's babies made her apprehensive about not having her own.

As weeks passed and her belly swelled, Neusa went on working. The housekeeper's resilience surprised Irina. They now saw each other only in passing. Irina's mother's deteriorating condition required that Irina visit her often. Neusa's arrival came to signal that Irina needed to head to the nursing home.

"Everything hurts," Neusa reported. "My back, my feet. I have terrible heartburn."

"Can I pay you not to work?" Irina joked one day, when the feeling of dread about seeing her mother overwhelmed her.

But also, she meant it. She wanted to do something to lighten Neusa's load. Twenty years into her life in Silicon Valley, Irina still couldn't believe the success she'd herself made. She was a lead engineer in a growing start-up. Evenings and weekends frequently found her in her home office, at the large white desk lit up by the three monitors. She owned her house. After her mother had gone into the nursing home, Irina redecorated in bursts of inspiration. She bought two expensive snake plants for her bedroom to improve the nighttime air quality. A professional wine fridge went into the kitchen. In her living room, she mounted a white board that doubled as a projector screen. Neusa came every Saturday morning to keep the surfaces shining.

Neusa gave her a look as though Irina was not making any sense. "My mother-in-law will help me next time. I'm training her to take over while I'm with the baby."

Irina blushed. She realized that if the sudden offer of unearned money had come to her from her boss, she would find it creepy, the opposite of a reward. She would suspect ulterior motives. Worst case scenario, she'd suspect her boss of wanting sexual favors. Even if not, it was like saying that the good job she'd been doing didn't matter and that she was being paid as a charity case. Americans, in Irina's experience, were skilled at negotiation—and though Neusa had grown up in Brazil, she'd come to the United States as a teenager. If Neusa wanted a change in her contract, she would say so.

In the car, thinking over the incident, Irina decided that next time, she would tell Neusa that she respected her professionalism and had made the offer as a friend. She had the extra money and would be glad to help.

That day, Irina found her mother looking gaunt, unable to leave her bed. She wouldn't speak English to the nurse and apparently had been refusing meals.

"When am I coming home?" her mother asked. "These people, they don't understand a word I'm saying."

"Do you want soup? It's mushroom barley today. Very nourishing."

Her mother agreed to swallow a spoonful. "You care about nobody but yourself. Where did I go wrong to raise such a cold-hearted daughter, tell me?"

Irina sighed.

Suddenly her mother leaned across the tray and whispered hotly. "There's a worker here—I think she wants to kill me. I've seen her look at me in a strange way. She found where I hide the money and took all of it. Now she thinks I have more. She's been trying to poison me."

"Nobody is trying to kill you, Mother," Irina said. She tried to ignore the wild look in her mother's eyes and speak calmly and steadily, as she'd seen the nurses do. "Your nurses make more money than you've ever had. They don't need your pennies."

Her mother allowed another spoonful of soup to be placed into her mouth, then shook her head. "Of course, they do. These people, they are greedy. They never have enough."

"These people? This is not Russia, Mother. You can't treat people who work for you as dirt. Everyone has equal rights in America. Did I tell you— my housekeeper, Neusa, she invited me to her baby shower. She's hosting this party—" The end of Irina's phrase hung in the air. She couldn't remember whether she'd finished buying the gift for the baby and, if the package had arrived, where she might've placed it. But wait, she recalled the date marked in sparkly blue letters at the top of the invitation, pinned to her bulletin board.

"What day is it today?" she asked, looking around the room. She pulled out her phone. How was it possible? The date had passed a week ago.

"Inform me when the President invites you to dinner," her mother said. "I would much rather your housekeeper made you soup."

Irina took a breath and exhaled what she always said to her mother. "In this country, nothing is impossible," Irina said. "Her son—you never know. He could grow up to become President."

"That's not how the world works. I'm sick of it," her mother said, pushing the tray away and spilling the rest of the soup.

Returning home that day, Irina found that Neusa had done as thorough a job on the house as ever, down to arranging the hand towels in her bathroom to look like flowers. In the kitchen, Neusa had taken the trouble to clean inside the fridge and to wipe the glass door of the wine fridge.

Irina arranged slices of cheese and apple on a plate and poured herself a glass of wine. Neusa would be as good a parent as she was a housekeeper. What hubris to think that Irina's mistake would matter in the long arc of this boy's life.

My Sister's Game

That July afternoon my sister Zoika was playing with our neighbor Artur as they did every night when it wasn't raining. I sat on a log and kept score. If a shuttlecock landed on the ground within a player's range, it counted as a miss.

I didn't always love my sister, but I loved watching her play with Artur. She was quick, her attention never wavered, and she could often predict Artur's sudden changes of speed and direction. Zoika was capable of bizarre physical feats, like flying sideways or falling to the ground and sliding across the dirt on her knees, with her racquet pushing forward. Her entire body reached up as she jumped for the high ones. Her braid flew high in the air behind her. I'd always wished for a braid like hers, but my own hair was too curly and the only way to manage it in the summer was to cut it as short as possible. I think she scored sometimes by mesmerizing Artur into a kind of a stupor. He admired her. He joked, sometimes, of being scared of her. Of course, Artur didn't have to try as hard. He was sixteen years old to her fifteen, and taller, more muscular. He could reach with his arm and hit the shuttle, and it went right back at Zoika, twisting her into the next move.

As the evening descended and the light paled, mosquitos rose from the grass. I felt a sting right beneath my ankle and another in the back of my neck. Swatting at the bugs with my racquet helped little. One hovered and hummed next to my head, and I couldn't shake it off. I stood up and began slicing the air. I couldn't stand mosquitos. But the idle exercise grew tiresome. I was itching everywhere and sweating.

We needed the rules to determine when to cut me in. Usually, Zoika let me switch places with her once in a while. But that evening she seemed to forget about me. The shadows were growing long. It wasn't like in June, when there was enough light to play until midnight. Soon, it would be too dark to see the shuttle.

"Play to win?" I asked.

Zoika shook her head. "Five more minutes."

"You've been saying that for hours!"

Artur was always eager to play competitively. No matter how many times he'd won against Zoika in the past, that didn't seem to diminish his pleasure. He winked at me. "Fifteen or twenty-one points?"

"Twenty-one," Zoika said.

"It's Marina's call," Artur insisted.

"Fifteen," I said.

Zoika was in particularly good form that day. I forgot about mosquitos for a few moments and stood still, watching her. But more than halfway through the set, when Zoika had only a few more rounds left to win, Katya from across the street showed up, her own racquet in hand. From the attic of her house, where she often hung out with her friends, she could see when we were out here, playing, so this was not accidental. Behind her, at some distance, loomed a few older kids. They were chatting and passing a bottle of alcohol around.

"Pairs?" Katya called out.

My sister hadn't seen her approach, and the voice startled her. She missed her serve.

"We're in the middle of a game." Zoika moved to serve again. I knew she didn't like Katya. She was Zoika's age, about fifteen, but she carried herself as a grown woman to Zoika's boyish ways. Zoika often made fun of the way Katya handled her racquet—it was as though she expected every shuttle to come to her, and she never reached for the shots that were coming in a little high or far to the side. As far as I was concerned, these quirks were useful. I liked to play with her—she made it easy for me to win. Zoika and Artur sometimes let me win, but with them, I always knew they were coddling to my age and size. At thirteen, I wasn't in the same league with them, and they made me feel it.

Artur remained motionless. There was always the question of where Artur's loyalties fell. "What's up with those guys?" he asked Katya.

"Serge and his friends want to join. The more, the merrier, isn't it? Serge has his guitar—"

Zoika's reaction was instant. "No! This is our game."

Katya continued to look at Artur, as though leaving the decision to him.

"All these guys do is smoke and drink. Why can't they go back to the burned-down store? That's a much better hangout for them," Zoika argued.

"They want to play. Are you afraid of them? I heard Serge say that he really likes you. He thinks you're shy, but I don't think that's true. Artur, what do you think?"

"I don't want to play with them." Zoika's voice went into higher pitch. I could see she was both angry and on the verge of tears. I felt bad for her. She was clearly backing herself into a position that she wouldn't be able to defend, and becoming angrier the more she recognized the futility of arguing further. Personally, I had nothing against Serge. His father had taken us fishing one summer, and though I hadn't caught anything, I had enjoyed the change in our routine. They'd had some kind of homemade liquor with them and, despite Zoika's protests, let me try a few sips. If Serge liked Zoika in any particular way, personally, I didn't see anything wrong with that.

"Sure," Artur began, but he didn't have time to formulate his opinion. Serge approached down the hill, and with him came another boy and two girls. A guitar hung over his shoulder, and even as he walked, his fingers strummed some kind of a melody.

"Can we watch for a bit?"

"We were in the middle of the game!" Zoika shouted.

"Go ahead and finish your game. Who's stopping you?" said one of the girls. She took a sip from the bottle of what was likely cheap vodka and passed it on to the other.

But it wasn't clear which game needed to be finished. We'd never settled into the pairs game; the game that Zoika had been playing against Artur was ancient history.

Zoika stepped back to the patch of grass we'd been using as our imaginary serve line and threw the shuttlecock in the air.

"How can you play badminton without a net?"

Badminton? But who really cared what the game was called. This had been our game. We played it the way we always did. The question had come from Vovka, the other boy in the group. I remembered him from the fishing trip. He was very handy. That day, though nobody had caught much, he'd been the one with the biggest haul: two gray spotted fish that he kept for his cat's dinner. But Zoika seemed to like him even less than Serge. She had that kind of expression, nearly a grimace, on her face, each time Vovka spoke.

"We're not playing professionally or anything," Artur said. "We're just fooling around."

"So, here's what you do." Vovka picked up a stick and started drawing the court lines. "The first rung of the ladder on that transformer booth is the bottom of the net, and the edge of the platform is the top. Any serve that goes in between is considered invalid."

"That's not how we play," Zoika said.

"Yes, but technically, Vovka is right. Haven't you seen last year's Olympics?" I knew she hadn't—but this was beside the point. Uttering these words, Artur chose a side against her.

Zoika struck the ground with her racquet, raising dust in the air.

"Somebody is having a bad day," one of the girls commented.

"You're only going to break it," Artur said. "Anyway, what's your problem? You're being such a girl! I didn't know you were even old enough to have PMS."

"I'm being a girl?"

The way Zoika repeated the words, it sounded like Artur had given her the ultimate put-down. A total betrayal. She swung her racquet at some weeds growing at the edge of our makeshift court with force enough that her braid flew across her shoulder and onto her chest. She yanked at the braid, as though trying to tear it off, but all she could do was push it behind her. Years later, I recall this moment vividly: I could tell how uncomfortable she was in her body; it wasn't Artur who had betrayed her as much as her own body, the body of a growing woman. The braid that our parents and grandparents praised so highly. I recall observing her discomfort in an impersonal way, as though it had nothing to do with me. I think at thirteen I still believed that Zoika's problems would never be mine.

She swung the racquet at the weeds again, shaving grass from its stems.

"You're going to ruin your racquet," Artur said, in an openly patronizing way. "This grass is very caustic."

She threw her racquet in his direction. Not at him, but close enough.

"You're crazy!"

She didn't answer, but yanked me by the hand and pulled me up the hill. "Never again," she repeated while she dragged me to our grandmother's house. "I hate him, I hate all of them."

It was pointless, trying to ask her "Why?" and "What do you have against Artur? Against Serge?"

"Marina, come! Zoika's in a mood, but you can stay," Artur called.

"I can teach you some chords," Serge said, strumming his guitar.

Zoika looked at me and squeezed my hand harder. I didn't protest.

She was behaving unreasonably, she wasn't fully in control of her emotions and their physical manifestations. She started crying, and I became fully convinced that something was really wrong with her. It took me many years and a lot of learning, intentional and accidental, to understand that moment as my first realization of Zoika's refusal to conform to the norms of her gender. She hated being a girl, but neither could she find a way to fit in among the boys of our neighborhood. She was okay hanging out with Artur, who for the most part treated her as a peer. But the other boys—that was different. I was just old enough to guess that, though I missed the specific signs, they must've expressed a sexual interest in her, and she couldn't stand it. What I knew for sure at that moment was that by staying by her side, I was forgoing an opportunity. Artur, Serge, Vovka—these were the people, the men, among whom my future lay, with whom I would have to learn how to deal as I grew up, in school, in the countryside. I knew that I needed to sidestep Zoika's grip and stay with them. But I couldn't do it. It wasn't because of Zoika, or it was only partially because of Zoika. I didn't want to.

I remember I kept glancing back as we walked up the hill, until Zoika pulled me around the corner. Serge picked up Zoika's racquet from the ground. They took positions, then Artur stepped back and hit the shuttle in a powerful serve.

"Net!" Serge shouted. He threw his arm forward, pointing, and it was as though I could truly see the net dividing the players. It was a strange experience. This was no longer my sister's game. Thinking back on those summer evenings spent playing together, I have to make a mental effort to remind myself that for a long time we'd been playing without the net.

Three Losses

Considering the chaotic life Jeanne led as a jazz singer, a show every god-damn night, Syd drinking bourbon with anyone who praised his keyboard skills, then at dawn cajoling him back to their home, and what a home it was—a Chinatown walk-up, seventh floor studio with a bathroom sink that also made do as a kitchen sink—after she broke up with Syd, a stream of men huffed and puffed up those stairs and held their sides from pain and collapsed on the sofa, sweating—considering all of that, and also that she managed to actually have a career, recording CDs, touring summers, taking an occasional week of downtime when she visited her mother in Syracuse, New York—taking it all into account, Jeanne's track record of keeping things together was remarkable.

One summer day, as she was returning from a gig in California, three losses came at once. She lost the baby—she thought of it as a baby, even though in the ninth week of pregnancy it was technically still only an em-bryo. At JFK airport, when she was almost home, somebody swiped the ukulele that she'd started using in her act after Syd left. Also, her thumb ring had disappeared. The ring simply vanished from her finger midflight. She was sitting on the airplane, listening to her iPod, trying to find solace in music between trips to the bathroom, and suddenly she noticed that her ring was gone. It had been a plain silver band, a trinket Syd picked up for her on the Atlantic City boardwalk once—literally picked it up from the ground and put on her finger. Unafraid of the pitying glances of the other passengers, she scoured the aisle, looked between the cushions, swept candy wrappers and foam headphone covers from under the seat. "Goddammit," she muttered to herself, "Goddamn Syd." A new cramp shot tears out of her eyes, and Jeanne collapsed to her elbows. A flight attendant came by with a cloying, patronizing look on her face, and helped Jeanne up and into her chair. "Next time, if you're not feeling well, it's best to delay your flight," she said.

Later, the doctor would explain that there was nothing she could've done to prevent the miscarriage. Most likely, her body eliminated the pregnancy because there was something wrong with the embryo. The wrong number of chromosomes, a genetic defect. The cells were dividing and multiplying, and then they weren't. On the plane, Jeanne bled heavily, and the cramps made her bite her lip and fist her hands, but still she was unable to hold back the tears. She hadn't decided whether or not to tell Syd about the pregnancy, and now there was nothing to tell. Syd had been hanging around her for over a decade, boozing every night and forcing her to be the responsible one and turning her into a witch. Jeanne decided there was a chance she'd swallowed the ring—she'd been in the habit of sucking on it at tense moments. Crouched in the tiny airplane bathroom, she looked for the ring in her stool, but couldn't see much in the water murky with blood clots.

When the plane landed at JFK, and she disembarked, a new wave of cramps and bleeding sent her to the bathroom again. Her body felt torn up inside, and when she felt the thing passing, she couldn't be sure whether it was the ring or the baby. She wiped and pulled up her pants, then went to wash her hands in the sink. That's when she noticed that somebody had taken her ukulele. She had dropped it off, together with her purse, on the counter near the hand towel dispenser. Her purse was still there, where she'd left it, but the black ukulele case had vanished, gone, and with it, the only thing Jeanne had bought for herself since Syd left. It was him she wanted back—the way he'd been when they first met, in Atlantic City, when after their gig, he took her down to the beach and threw handfuls of sand at the stars and told her he loved her.

Jeanne stood for a while over the sink, staring at her hands—when she looked in the mirror she could see four of them—they were large hands with calloused, strong fingers and bulging red knuckles, and a little dent where her thumb ring had been. She washed her face, picked up her purse and went out into the steamy, sweltering New York afternoon to find a cab. She had a gig that evening. She had to keep it together for at least one more night.

A Bear's Tune

As we finish off the tarragon chicken Abby prepared for dinner, she turns the conversation toward her sister's upcoming wedding. I'd much rather continue talking about Abby's middle-school student who refuses to participate in group work, or move on to watching *Orange Is the New Black*—we have just enough time to watch an episode before Abby's bedtime. It's Sunday. This evening was supposed to be reserved for the two of us, connecting. But, earlier today, Abby finally reached her sister on the phone. The good news: I'm invited to Kathleen's wedding as Abby's girlfriend and "significant other."

Scheduled for a weekend in mid-July, the wedding promises to be massive. Kathleen runs the credit card customer service at a large department store and the guy she's going to marry manages an entire mall in Allentown, PA—the town where Abby grew up and where most of her family still lives. Abby's already calculated the cost of two airplane tickets from San Francisco to Philadelphia and the car rental to drive up to Allentown for the weekend. She'd prefer to go for an entire week, or even two, but she's scheduled to teach camp for the whole month of July. It has to be just the weekend.

"I've been thinking, I should go visit Sarra Naumovna," I tell Abby. We're sitting in our San Francisco apartment, the kitchen table cluttered with my law books, Abby's laptop, keyboard, and mouse, dirty plates piled with chicken bones, and two large wine glasses newly refilled.

"Sarah who?"

"Sarra Naumovna. You know!"

She looks at me.

"My father's solfeggio teacher," I say.

"I'm sorry—I'm drawing a blank."

"The person I was staying with when you and I first met!"

My words fail to penetrate the distant look on her face. Abby and I have been together for six-and-a-half years and, apparently, that's both too long and not long enough.

"If you want to visit this person, I'm not stopping you. But it's not cool if you want to go during my sister's wedding." Abby helps herself to another slice of store-bought apple pie, my contribution to the meal.

"I can skip the bachelorette party."

"You can't miss my sister's bachelorette's party!"

"Look, I don't do femme. My bar exam is at the end of July. Actually, it's insane for me to even be going anywhere at this time." The reality of this hits me as the words roll off my tongue. There are five short months between now and July. When I visualize my calendar, the stress makes the wine blister in my throat. I want to be lying in bed already, cradled in Abby's soft body. I glance at the microwave clock: 10:42 p.m. It's always five minutes ahead, though.

"Masha, you have to come with me to the party. Kathleen specifically asked me if you were coming, and I told her you were." Abby punctuates her speech by taking a large piece of the pie into her mouth. She swallows without chewing. Can she taste anything but the sugar? She probably wishes she'd made the dessert. The store-bought stuff never fills her craving.

"She won't miss me. The party's for her friends. I've met her exactly twice."

"Kathleen's friends are the people who made my life miserable in high school. They thought I was a weirdo then, and now probably more so. Imagine, I'm in my mid-thirties, and I teach inner-city kids and live in a tiny apartment with some chick! I don't have money for a manicure and a hair treatment! I am fifty pounds overweight and still wear shirts with horizontal stripes. This is, like, the exact horror scenario they warn their kids against."

"This isn't how you see yourself, is it?"

"Don't leave me. I don't want to do this alone!"

"You can always dazzle them with the conversation about sheet thread counts and credenzas. Remember that time when Kathleen flew in for a conference, and we had martinis at the Top of the Mark? She loved what you had to say on the subject of living room decor. She appreciates your sense of humor. Look, it's not like I'm saying I won't go to the wedding."

"Don't be like this. Kathleen isn't perfect, but she's my only sister. I want to be there for her."

"And Sarra Naumovna is old. She has dementia."

"I don't see how that's relevant to what we're talking about."

"Really? You're telling me what's important to you. I'm reminding you about the fact that I have different priorities. I haven't seen Sarra Naumovna in—it's been much too long. She survived the Leningrad blockade . . . She has these crazy stories about making soup from glue sticks and boiling pine needles for tea." I catch my distorted reflection in the nearly empty wine glass. The bottom of my face looks broad, my chin three times its size. If I want more wine, I have to start a new bottle. The effort seems like too much. I'll let Abby make the call.

"One day you'll have to explain what that means. What I hear now is that you don't think Kathleen is interesting enough. But go ahead and talk some more about our difference in values, or whatnot. You're the lawyer!"

Abby's lack of interest about my Russian background used to seem endearing. How many people, including my college girlfriend, tried, through me, to access something they thought they admired. Oh, Russia: ballet, figure skating, Tchaikovsky, Tolstoy, Dostoyevsky, Fabergé eggs. I'd started to identify with the children of celebrities, when casual strangers ask them, But what are your famous parents really like? Abby has never been like that. With her, it's like she'd never even heard the name of my country before we met, and now that she's placed it on the map, she doesn't care. She loves me because of who I am.

"First, I'm not a lawyer and I won't be unless I pass the bar. Second, no, this has nothing to do with your sister. I mean, yes, she's boring. But that's not the point. Sarra Naumovna—she was the one who introduced my father to *Jesus Christ Superstar*. One of her former students smuggled the Broadway soundtrack to the Soviet Union. Because of her, my father fell in love with rock opera. Because of her he decided to emigrate . . . "

"Are you somehow laughing at me?" Abby puts down her fork.

I stop. "You're right. This is probably more sad than funny. You should see Sarra Naumovna's apartment. It's like being back in Leningrad. It's tiny, but of course, there's the upright piano. And the books! She has these old scores from Broadway musicals that she brought from the Soviet Union. They had been so hard to obtain that she couldn't imagine parting with them, even though she was going to New York! You really should come."

"Plan a trip to Allentown after your exam. If this woman is so important to you."

Abby stands and gathers the dishes. She sweeps the chicken bones off the plates and loads the dishwasher, extra cautious to avoid banging sounds. I should help put away the leftovers. The remaining slice of the pie goes in the fridge—or does it stay on the counter? Does Abby mean to eat it tonight? She hasn't finished her wine. When she's in this mood, I can't do anything right by her.

What she said must sound so logical to her. Either do this, or that. Make a decision. Buy a ticket and go. If you can't make the time, well then, it wasn't that important in the first place. I've been trying to keep to this program, but here's what happens: the stupid nonsense of our everyday lives always takes precedence, and the things that matter, that really matter, are left behind. The image of my calendar keeps pressing on my mind. It's a complicated computer matrix with my work schedule and study schedule in pink and orange and the appointments from Abby's calendar showing up in blue. To cram in a night like this, just for the two of us, we had to plan a month in advance. We're not using the time well.

I finish my wine and say, "It's easy for you to say, go. You forget that I don't drive. By bus from Philly, it takes half a day." Yeah, I'm bitter. What Abby probably hears is *whaa-whaa-whaa-whaa*. If she can hear anything behind the running water.

Sarra Naumovna was in her seventies in 2003, that summer when I graduated from Temple in Philadelphia and went to live with her in Allentown. I'd been thinking of going back to Russia. My parents were horrified. They'd pleaded with me to find a job instead. Finally I'd struck a bargain with them. They would pay for my international airfare if I learned to be a better Russian before I returned. I took a menial job in Sarra Naumovna's building, cleaning the apartments. Most residents were Russian-speaking, hailing from the far reaches of the former Soviet Union. The job's physical and social aspects tired me out. I had to not only wash the floors and clean the crummy kitchens and bathrooms, but to hear the residents tell me that I was doing everything wrong and instruct me on how to properly bend my back, in which direction to slide my mop, the way to dispose of the dirty water.

In the evenings, Sarra Naumovna treated me to Russian-style meals, massive three-course affairs starring dill and parsley in every dish. Many of her friends in the building would cram at the dinner table. When the tea was served, the hostess sat at the piano. Before Leningrad, she'd lived in Belorussia, and she knew classical and popular Russian, Yiddish, Belorussian, Ukrainian, German music. Her friends, mostly women about the same age or older, asked for songs they could sing together. Folk songs and bard songs and songs from musicals and TV movies; there were humorous songs and songs written during wartime and in labor camps, full of obscene jargon that in Sarra Naumovna's rendition never seemed truly offensive. Each song led into a story, and from each story emerged another song. Once Sarra Naumovna started singing, she couldn't be stopped until after nine p.m.— by the rules of the building, the quiet hour.

When at the end of three months with Sarra Naumovna, I finally did return to St. Petersburg, I caught a flu right away, was groped in the subway, and my attempt at registering at a local public library was stone-walled by the librarian who pretended not to understand my questions. I was back in the United States within a month. Nothing in contemporary Russia corresponded with the world that I'd glimpsed in Allentown.

I've stayed in telephone contact with Sarra Naumovna. Before I left the East Coast, I visited her often, including that one memorable trip when I met Abby at a woman-owned bar in Allentown. A few years ago, something changed. When I called Sarra Naumovna one evening, she didn't recognize my voice right away. "Who did you say you were? What are you calling about?" I started to suspect that she was developing dementia. It's been months now, about five or six, since I talked to her. Now would be the time to visit, to thank her, to tell her how much she has meant to me. But does she even know what's happening to her? Is she scared? I'm not sure if she can still play the piano. What if she can't?

Pushing the piece of pie back and forth on its plate, I wait for Abby to say something. I should go brush my teeth and put on my pajamas and heat the little rice pillow she likes to keep near her feet when she's falling asleep, but her silence holds me in place. I keep hoping she'll turn from the dishwasher and say something like, "I'm sorry. I know your Russian friends are important to you. This wedding thing doesn't have to be an either-or thing. Let's figure out how we can do both."

She finishes her wine and goes to the bathroom, passing by without looking at me. When she's really mad, Abby defaults to her routines. She flosses diligently in front of the mirror, brushes front to back for exactly two minutes, washes her face with cold water, applies soothing cream, pees, flushes, washes her hands, dries, moves to the bedroom. I wish there were a way for me to explain Sarra Naumovna to her.

There's nothing to do but to follow Abby to the bedroom.

"I love you. I want to make you happy," I say. "Tell me what's so important about this bachelorette party. This is one night, one thing I'm asking for," I beg.

Abby is still too upset to talk. She goes through her closet, picks out her outfit for the day ahead. A polka dot shirt that the kids love. The pants with a stretchy band that she wears when she feels extra heavy. I've noticed she's been avoiding the scale. When she feels good about her body, she weighs herself in the mornings and in the evenings. I glance at the clock: 11:08. A yawn comes. From it, the fear emerges. A full-blown fight could take us to one, two o'clock in the morning. I need to have a fresh head tomorrow. A partner I want to impress invited me to sit in on a new client meeting. If I do well—this could make or break my career with this firm.

Sarra Naumovna, I think. Her head of orange-henna-colored hair floats above the keys, and her pale blue eyes are fixed on me. There was no air-conditioning in her unit, as in most units of that building, and in the evenings the place was like a Turkish bath. I remember having to strip down to a tiny tank top during work hours. I remember sitting on Sarra Naumovna's couch, drinking tea, and sweating, sweat pouring down my forehead and stinging my eyes. The elderly women complained about the heat, and still closed the windows at night against the "drafts." The nights made me feel like I ran a hundred degree fever. In the mornings, I woke up smelling sour and stale, my back aching, my arms feeling like I'd pulled myself up a cliff. How and when in my life did I start thinking of my summer at Sarra Naumovna's as a positive experience? I'm not even particularly fond of music. My father used to say—a Russian expression—that a bear must've stepped on my ear when I was a child. I can't tell when somebody's off key.

I sit on my side of the bed, reveling in the coolness and softness of its sheets, in the comfort of the blackout blinds that Abby insisted we splurge on for our windows. I was upset with her today for killing most of the afternoon on her cooking project, but I know how much she enjoys cooking. This is one of the myriad of ways in which she makes our house into a home. I love this about her.

"Fine, I'll skip Sarra Naumovna's. If it's so important to you, I'll go with you. But you'll need to explain how you want me to be with those bachelorettes. Do I turn up the gay? Do I try to fit in? What?"

Abby starts crying. Somehow I've missed a clue. "What? What?" She doesn't say. She climbs onto the bed with her shoes on and rocks herself, crying. I stand there, in front of her, my arms hanging down. I'm scared. I don't know, I have no idea what more she needs right now and what the big deal is. I mean, I've just offered her everything.

Plastic Film with a Magnetic Coating

I'm thinking that in addition to other things, we've been failing to teach and learn the language of desire. I remember how, as a fifteen-year-old girl, listening to the Beatles, I thought my life was going to be a disaster because I'd never, ever be able to express my feelings to a boy—the very act of speaking up in that way would ruin any chances I had with that boy. If I spoke, I would immediately become a woman who speaks first, aka who speaks too much, and, in that very instance, I would stop being an object of desire. The Beatles could sing about holding hands but I didn't even have the courage to put this song on a mix tape for my boys. I stuck with milder, less personal songs. "Lucy in the Sky with Diamonds." "I Am the Walrus." Who could figure out what these songs were about? The guys, as far as I could tell, had a different kind of problem. They were encouraged to speak, but they didn't have the words. Speaking words of endearment to a girl wasn't an option because words of endearment coming out of a boy's mouth automatically made him less boy, less male. To be masculine, the boys had to say something like, "you're a bitch"—and that would be a clear signal to a girl that she was an object of interest. Of course, a touchy girl could be put off by this kind of come-on; that was the risk the boys had to take. So, the boys, too, came to consider the Beatles and the mix tapes. The trouble was, tapes cost a lot of money back then and not everyone had the equipment, so there were many third parties involved in the mix tape transaction—the messages frequently got mixed up. I'm speaking, of course, of a very different time and place.

Ada at Twelve and a Half

There she is at 8:35 in the morning on her way to school: Ada, a tall, earth-brown-haired girl. There, there she is, walking out the door, exactly on time. The cold northwestern wind throws wet cherry blossoms at her face, twists last year's leaves into the viscous sky between the two apartment blocks. A car's ignition starts and breaks off, starts again, holds. Fuming up the neighborhood, the neighbor drives away.

Ada looks back. She wants to shrink inside the house.

Blocking the threshold, her mother stands warmly wrapped in pajamas and a robe. "Go on, Adassa," Mother says in the private language she and Ada share, the language foreign to this country. She uses Ada's full name, as she does when she wants to be obeyed. She gives Ada a little push on the shoulders. "I won't be home today; have lunch at school."

The door closes behind Ada. From outside, the brown clapboard apartment building where Ada and her mother live looks identical to the adjacent unit, to all the houses in this development. The black, brown, or gray doors stare with fish-eye peepholes as Ada creeps past them. She rounds the corner.

Six hundred seventy-six steps separate Ada from school. It's a straight path that takes her past the primary school and the playground, past the Alzheimer's residential facility across the road, then down past the church and the cemetery with tall weathered stone crosses. After the church, the athletic fields open, and then there's the middle school, a prominent building, in front of which hundreds of girls in identical uniforms will already be assembling.

Ada's backpack weighs heavily on her shoulders. The power of the way things are in the world propels her toward the school. Mary Poppins won't be dropping by to rescue her. No prince is parading on his horse in search for his true love. No creepy child kidnappers are lurking by the playground. There are no explosives hidden behind that hedge up on the left. The earth won't open up to swallow her this morning. Nothing will stop Ada from going to school this and every morning until summer break. The devastating truth is: it's an average day in an average suburb of Boston and Ada, though she doesn't belong here, is an average girl to whom only average things happen. She has a long life ahead of her. The walk to school is only the beginning.

The primary school is busy this time of day. Cars pull up to the curb and parents take their children by the hand and deliver them to the doors of a squat yellow building prettily painted with elephants and giraffes. The primary school Ada had attended a sea and light-years east of here was far less cheerful. These kids are bright-eyed and clean. "Look, there are all your friends," one red-haired mother tells her red-haired little girl, and the girl leaves the mother's side and joins the children running in circles around the wet playground. The mother stands back, watching, smiling. There must be a comfort in being taken to school by a parent—there's no pretense of choice. Ada is allowed to go to school on her own because at twelve-going-on-thirteen, she's considered old enough and responsible enough to get there, and, of course, she will get there.

The interminable day ahead looms. The thought of the dank school cafeteria churns in her guts, threatens to dislodge the morning's porridge. She cannot take another step toward the school. She doesn't have the power to stop going. She turns her face up into the wind: if only the wind helped her grow faster, cut the baby fat from her cheeks, lengthened her bones, solidified her features, made her beautiful. She has read books in which pitiful girls grew up to be important women. Her eyes might even change color from plain brown to green or blue. If only she had green eyes, the next step would be easier. She imagines herself drawn in glitter, a princess twirling through the pages of a picture book. Her fantasy sparks—and vanishes, sinks in the memory of the place where she and her mother had come from, the land of skinny, naked birch trees drowning in mud. Thick and oily, it's the kind of mud that slurps hungrily when you take a step, that fills the spaces under your fingernails and in your ears, and when it dries on your skin and hair, it forms a mold and has to be scraped off with a knife.

Ada's fingernails are squeaky-clean. The straps of her backpack are starting to cut into her shoulders.

Across the road stands a stone building with columns that houses people with advanced Alzheimer's disease. Nurses and doctors care for them and, Ada imagines, researchers investigate the nature of their condition. All the doors and windows are closed, and the building looks like a fortress walled off by a tall green hedge. The yard is empty now, but, in the afternoons, patients who can still walk traverse the lawn. Their backs stooped and legs infirm, they move slowly, hanging on to their nurses' arms, glumly staring at the ground ahead. Ada is aware that there's no escape from the fortress. "What if—they wanted to be by themselves?" she asked her mother once.

"But they don't," Mother said.

"But what if?"

"These people don't want anything anymore."

Ada knows what she wants, but what choice does she have? She takes another step forward. She could stop. She can.

Up ahead there's a crossroad, and the girls in blue plaid skirts and blue sweaters are gathering from neighboring streets. Ada's skirt, bought with growth in mind, comes down to her ankles. Her blue sweater hangs on her like a toga, and underneath she's wearing a beige T-shirt. The regulation white button-down is in the laundry basket, and there was some argument this morning about whose fault it was, Ada's or her mother's, that the shirt remained unwashed. Which of the Emmas or Chloes in her class will be the first today to point out this obvious fact, that Ada's wearing the wrong shirt? Will the reprimand come from one of the teachers, a counselor, the principal? Ada, they think, doesn't understand their language, and she has this advantage—she can refuse to understand their language, though what's not to understand? A uniform is a uniform is a uniform.

Here's the church, a tall building with a steeple erected from the same time-defying stone as the Alzheimer's facility across the street. The Catholic girls come here to pray every Sunday. Once Ada went in with them and stood in the back, watching as they kneeled and rose and repeated words and gestures as if they were puppets in the theater. The solemn expressions they pinned to their faces mirrored that of the man on the cross, hanging over the altar. But the moment they took their seats, Ada glimpsed how the girls made faces at one another behind their parents' backs. Ada wondered what made them go through with this routine that seemed so removed from anything real. There was no point in looking for a friend among these girls. As they started chanting again, she backed away through the door.

The church is where Adassa stops.

Beyond the church lie the cemetery and the school's brand new turf and track field. She hasn't seen anyone from her class yet, but if she walks any further, the meeting is unavoidable. If she is to disappear, she has to disappear now.

She stands still, shuddering in the wind. The door of the church is open, and she can't help staring into the cavernous interior. In that darkness, as if reading her future in the coffee grounds, Ada, at twelve and a half years old, glimpses the entire arc of her life, and it pivots on this very moment: what will she do next?

A small crow jumps from the hedge and onto the church step. It opens its beak and makes a loud groaning sound. The bird takes a few anxious steps and, suddenly spooked by something or someone, flies away, black swath against the gray sky.

Behind the church, at the back of the cemetery, there's a secluded alley where three luxuriant lilac bushes are in full bloom. In the evenings, when her mother is on the computer, working, always working, Ada likes to sneak outside and sit on the grass beneath the lilacs. Time moves imperceptibly there, stayed by the very purple of the garlands of flowers, by their intoxicating fragrance. The cold seems more bearable. Lying beneath the lilacs, she absorbs the wetness of grass, allowing ants to crawl on her body and through her hair, feeling the drops of dew condense on her face without wiping them off. She longs to stay there forever, but never lasts more than a quarter of an hour. Later, back inside the apartment, shivering in their large and drafty room where the radiator is never more than lukewarm, she starts longing for the lilacs again.

Ada takes two steps in the direction of the cemetery and the lilac bushes, bites her lip, and recalling the warnings and admonishments she's been given about tardiness, returns to her school-bound path. She doubts whether this is the right decision, or if this is a decision at all. She only knows that, from the moment she left her house, it was inevitable that she gets to school, and in a few dozen steps, she will pass through the school gate, bump shoulders with a girl who will look down to her, will make her way across the broad, overcrowded hallway to the classroom where she will sit, trying, and failing, to accept the ordinary.

Like Water

I'm nearly forty-two and happily married. Two children. We live in a university town in Southern California, where my husband is a tenured professor of Atmospheric Science and I am an adjunct in the Foreign Languages and Literatures department. I teach undergraduate courses in Russian Literature and Culture. Which is to say, even though I left the Soviet Union almost thirty years ago, my heritage still takes up the greater part of who I am. When asked, where are you from? I invariably answer, Leningrad.

I was fifteen when my parents brought me, against my will, to the Bronx. Most people are confused by the "against my will" part. They assume everyone wanted out of Russia. But how does one explain one's home? The only way I know is to tell the stories.

Imagine: You're sitting in the back row of a Leningrad theater that once was a palace a long, long time before your birth, but now half of the chairs are broken, the plaster is peeling from the ceiling, sections of the balcony railing are missing, and as the performance begins, the curtain catches and a workman in blue overalls comes out to yank it open. You're fifteen. The friend sitting on your left you've known since you were ten, the one on the right since you were six. The outing to see *Eugene Onegin* is a school thing. You've studied the Pushkin novel. You and most of your classmates are familiar with the opera—it airs on TV several times a year. On stage, the soprano confesses her love for the baritone. She's in her boudoir, a faithful reconstruction of a 19th century country house such as you might find in the Pavlovsk Palace, sans the fourth wall. Tatiana writes a letter to Eugene, with whom she's fallen in love. She dwells on the moment of their first meeting: Eugene is a rare visitor from the capital and charms her by his very presence. In starts and fits she describes her passion; she alternates between blessing and cursing her fate. She's aware that she's trespassing the mores of the day by so openly confessing her love and begs him for understanding. You know that this is going to end badly for her, and yet there's a moment when the Tchaikovsky score swoops you up and fills your heart with hope for Tatiana.

Suffering, aching, the singer throws her feather pen on the desk—and the desk collapses. The whole bedroom set crashes magnificently around her, the walls, by pure luck, falling away from the singer. Dust rises from the stage. Unflinching, the soprano finishes the aria, declaiming her trust in the baritone to be absolute.

In the back row, your friend on the left is laughing so hard, the chair gives way beneath her. The seat comes off its hinges and falls to the floor, and she falls with it, causing a ruckus—and a renewed bout of laughter. What a disaster! What a treat. An opera, so dead that it's literally falling to pieces, is suddenly turned into a masterful art form as the singers' voices soar above the ruin, struggling to communicate the ineffable something to a multitude of teenage barbarians gathered in the dark.

And yet even as a fifteen-year-old I knew that the joy my friends and I shared was the other side of terror, born of the spectacle of degradation and loss. A star bursts, an empire falls, a ball of fire streaks across the sky. For us, its witnesses, this could be a once-in-a-lifetime event. This could also be the start of the blaze that would consume our lives. The year was 1990. The future, impossible to tell.

*   *   *

Today is June 9th, 2017. A few days ago, there was a meme going around social media, in which people recalled moments in their lives when they laughed the hardest. In honor of Pushkin's birthday, I posted that story from the Leningrad theater—I did my best to keep it brief to match the medium, yet described the scene in some detail for my American friends. Many of my colleagues love to hate social media, but, personally, I find it useful for keeping in touch with my friends in faraway places. It's been particularly so in the last few years, after my husband and I moved away from the East Coast and found ourselves in the traffic-choked Californian suburbs.

I was gratified when my friends, those who had shared the experience with me, saw my post and commented on it. Katya wrote first—she said, "It's a wonder I wasn't hurt when that chair fell! I did pick up a splinter from holding on to the armrest so hard. We were lucky to escape from that theater alive." Katya, now a lawyer, has become increasingly nervous over the years. She's had a difficult life. Shortly after university, she married one of our classmates, had a daughter, divorced, and married another classmate. With him, she also had a daughter. Both girls are named Eugenia. If I had to guess, Katya allowed each of her husbands to pick the name. She doesn't find this funny. I presume there's no specific connection to *Eugene Onegin*.

Tanya, my friend from kindergarten, the one who was on my right during the show, became a botanist and married a colleague from Norway. She's a mycologist who lives above the Arctic Circle. Her daughter, a year younger than my eldest, turns sixteen this year. Tanya, too, commented on my post. She wrote, "I remember that day so well! You kept making me laugh. I can't remember what you found so funny, but I was enamored of the casual way you treated something as solemn as *Onegin*. That was the moment I fell in love with you."

When I read this comment, the hair at the back of my neck stood up.

"How do you mean this?" I typed.

She responded eight hours later, no thanks to time zones. "I mean it," she said.

"Please, say more."

"I don't know if there's more. We can talk about it in person one day."

What the hell was Tanya talking about? She'd said something, and then said it again, yet her words left me completely confused.

I've been sitting in front of my computer for three days straight, grading student work and browsing social media, trying to lose myself among other people's stories. My husband and children have gone on a camping trip to a small canyon lake, and I have the house to myself—if not my mind. I've corrected one hundred Russian adjectives to the proper declension. I've worked on two hundred verbs, to fix their conjugation and aspect. I'm completely caught up on the latest gossip about the Trump and Putin bromance.

Tanya—could she possibly be talking of having had physical interest, of desiring me in body and spirit? Why would she be confessing this now, and following such a random prompt? Perhaps what she means is simply that she loves me as a friend. Which isn't news. Sure, I love her too. We are friends—we've been friends all these years. We've had the opportunity to reminisce about our childhood and to bond over Katya's increasing strangeness. Personally, I'm still hung up on Katya naming both of her daughters Eugenia. What a way to brand the girls with their mother's insufficiently examined past.

All I can do, it seems, is to sit here and stare, at the churning engine of history. Tanya. She must've meant it casually. But the longer I think about it, the more moments from our past emerge—the occasional touch, the look, the unexpectedly tender word—that could've been interpreted differently. I recall a fiction she and I had composed together, about the three of us, Katya, Tanya, and me, building a house on a remote island in the North Sea and living there together, fishing and picking mushrooms and berries. She drew maps of the island, and I designed the house. I remember finding it strangely appropriate when Tanya went on her first expedition to the Arctic. I knew she must've had that old story in the back of her mind.

I call Tanya on Skype, looking at her profile snapshot as my computer simulates the dial tone. She's lost a lot of weight in her middle age. There had always been something birdlike in her profile, and lately, her features have become sharper, more definite. She doesn't answer. Is she busy? Is she avoiding this conversation? Both, I decide. As an experiment, I imagine caressing her lips with mine, touching her body through the sweaters she's always wearing. In my mind, her face expresses pleasure and longing at my touch.

I hang up and turn off my computer, and go to the living room, where I turn the TV on and off. It's midafternoon and going outside is off limits—too hot. This Californian desert seems like a particularly grotesque place to be right now. And yet it's home. The kids are coming home tonight and they expect me to quiz them on their adventure.

Did Tanya really mean girl-on-girl love? Could she have?

This feels crazy. At the age of forty-two, I have the honor to consider, for the first time, what my life might have been like, were I aware, at the age of fifteen, that women did not need to marry men. That they could love each other and live with each other and raise children with each other. What would my life have been like if I'd heard of a woman openly living with another woman? If I'd met women raising children together? If I'd known a single person who responded to women caught loving women with anything other than "This is a phase," and "She's a freak," and "How disgusting," and "That poor thing"?

A half-forgotten image from 1990 emerges. A memory of something I'd glimpsed? A vivid fantasy? A jumbled movie track? Two girls, sucking each other's tongues in the dark, barely heated entryway of an unfamiliar apartment building. Becoming so weak in the knees that they collapse onto the concrete stairs, and startling each time they hear a noise from behind the doors up the stairwell. They seek each other's closeness as protection from possible intrusion. Jamming into each other's breasts. Twisting the nipples. Trying to navigate the folds of winter clothing to locate each other's clits.

And then what? From that entryway, they go—where? Do they hold hands? Do they keep seeing each other? Imagining what girl love must've looked like back then is like trying to construct a fucking parallel universe. I know—I've heard some stories since then—I know some girls got away with this. I still don't know how they had the guts to attempt it.

*　　*　　*

Here's a story. Once upon a time, circa 1993, there lived an elderly couple, who'd recently immigrated from the Soviet Union, following their children and grandchildren. They lived in a small apartment in the Bronx and suffered from many ailments. The husband had weathered three heart attacks and several bouts of kidney stones. The wife had debilitating arthritis and osteoporosis. Their health insurance allowed them one medical checkup a year. They tackled the checkup appointment together. The doctor was a middle-aged woman, about the same age as their daughter. Talking through a translator, the couple began their litany of complaints.

The doctor interrupted them. "Here's what you're going to do," she said. "Each of you has to drink two liters of water a day. This will alleviate your symptoms. Make sure it's not soda. Not juice. Not coffee or tea. Water, plain and simple."

"But, listen, doctor," they protested.

"I encounter this problem often with my immigrant population, where people come from places with bad water. People don't drink enough—especially the elderly. Go home and drink, drink, drink. I'll see you next year."

They looked at each other and sighed. They'd heard the rumors of the quality of American medicine, but they hadn't expected anything this bad.

The next year, they went to see a different doctor. A young man, looking tired, but disposed to listen. He nodded thoughtfully, they thought. The couple concluded their tale with the absurd advice they'd received from the previous doctor. The young fellow's face brightened. "Did you follow my colleague's recommendation?" he asked.

"What? She played a joke on us."

"The research is solid on this. Most people need to consume at least sixteen ounces of clear liquids per day. At least!"

"What are clear liquids?"

"Water, juice. Plain water is best."

"What about tea?"

"No tea. Tea has the opposite effect—it's a diuretic."

"We could try taking our tea with milk."

"What you need is plain water. Don't you drink water?"

"We've been drinking black tea our entire lives. The taste of water makes us queasy."

"What about bottled water? It has no taste."

"Waste money on water? You're out of your mind."

"Well—you could squeeze a little lemon in your water. Add some cucumber slices. Find a way. Trust me, it's good for you."

"Yes, yes. Americans think that water is a panacea against each and every disease. Fine. Since we can't receive proper treatment, we'll be dead all the sooner."

"I don't know what to tell you. You don't have any acute symptoms at this time, do you?"

"But, doctor, we will."

"This is your prescription. See? I'm writing this down: bib. 16 oz. aqua o.d. Omni diem—that means, every day. Come back next year—and we'll talk about what else you can do."

The elderly couple didn't see any options. Walking home hand in hand, they made a pact to follow the doctor's orders.

This is what they did. They started with a single mug. After their evening tea, the wife emptied the boiled water from the kettle into a large mug and placed the mug in the center of the table. Over the course of the following day, as the two of them moved about their apartment, making and eating the day's meals, taking the pills their friends and family members brought from the former Soviet Union, reading the newspaper, watching TV—whatever they were doing—the mug of water stared them down. Once in a while, one of them dared to take a sip. Then the other had to take a sip, too. That had been their deal. This way, little by little, daring and provoking each other, by the end of the day, they usually managed to drain the mug to the last drop.

The next year, they returned to see the doctor. He was young, but at the very least, he took the trouble of hearing them out. "We did what you told us to do," they said. "We drank the water."

"And?"

"And what do you think? It's water."

"Describe exactly what you did."

They told him about the mug in the middle of the table, and how much effort it took them to finish it each day.

"I don't understand," the young doctor said. "We live in a world made predominantly of water. Sixty percent of the human body consists of water. Our cells need water to function. How is it that you could've lived such long lives and not learned that water is the basic ingredient that humans need?"

The husband and the wife looked at each other. Both of them had tears in their eyes. "You speak with passion, young man," they said to the doctor. "We appreciate this passion. There might be some truth to what you're saying. But we're afraid your advice comes too late. Water is not for us. We drink tea."

*   *   *

Here's the point. Like my grandparents, I, too, have been born to a world made of water. Here, in the arid part of Southern California, where we have barely ten inches of rain a year, this point has been brought home to me. I had never paid enough attention to the water.

I keep rereading the message Tanya left me, "That was the moment I fell in love with you," and my heart is palpitating, and I feel so close—like

I'm about to understand something important. I'm fifteen—I'm watching *Eugene Onegin*—Tatiana's writing her letter—the stage set collapses, and—

I picture Tanya's laughing face turned to me, and past the laughter, the questioning, searching look in her eyes. But what do I know. That was thirty years ago. I try again—

My imagination fails. My parents come and sweep me off to New York.

I look up the cost of airfare to Tromsø, Norway. I could buy a ticket to visit Tanya—sure I have my kids, and my classes to teach, and dissertations to supervise, and conference panels to plan. I have my husband, who has been a steady partner for more than fifteen years, and who relies on me to put in my share of housework and childcare.

It takes twenty-two hours to reach Tanya's town from my own.

If I were to fly to Norway, Tanya has her life. A house to manage, her children, her collection of fungi. It would come down to a series of awkward moments. "I love you too," ending with a cursory hug and a kiss on the cheek.

And most likely, it's too late. My habits have been too firmly established. Water isn't for me. But I'm staring at the mug—it's right there in the middle of the table. I can't forget that water is in there. I've grown used to something else by now, but what if I dared? What if I did what so many of my students do at eighteen or twenty? Namely, experiment. Try out a new identity. I'm terrified, but I also can't pretend I don't understand. Water is life.

Gift Exchange

An office holiday party gift triggers this memory. Sasha was in her early twenties, working an entry level data analyst job, when she and her co-worker Jamie frequented a kitchenware store to have their laughs. This was back in Boston, before Sasha moved to Oakland. During lunch-break, Sasha and Jamie would ride the elevator to the ground floor, cross the street, and start giggling as they approached the storefront, with the name of the place affixed over the entrance in loopy metal lettering. "Because we're so *French*, we *must* use cursive script. Print is so lowbrow!"

It was Jamie who always played the jester, but Sasha had no trouble keeping up. She'd immigrated with her parents from the Soviet Union a few years before, and couldn't fathom ever needing more than a sharp knife and frying pan for cooking her meals.

The store greeted them with bouquets of spatulas and trees of oven mitts. "You should buy the American flag mitt for your left hand, and the French for your right. Then your *baguette* will come out undercooked on the inside and burned on the outside."

"*Exactement!* Just the way I like it!" The two of them found this sort of banter murderously funny and could keep it going for hours. All the graters and the slicers, each shaped for a specific fruit or vegetable, extravagant tools for opening jars and cans, the molds for frying or microwaving eggs—oh what fun it was to imagine the pretentious, self-important people who would find these things indispensable.

Sasha still remembered Jamie's impersonation of the gesticulating hostess. Jamie cocked her head and smiled that saccharine smile of American TV chefs. "Allow me to infuse a few slivers of lemon peel into your bourbon with this lemon-colored *zester*, because everyone knows that good bourbon tastes like Schnapps without that scrape of lemon peel! No, no, you mustn't use the lime-colored thing—zester, I mean—lest your lemon turns into lime." Hours of fun.

Jamie, a music student, quit that tedious data analyst job in a matter of weeks. "My humanity's languishing! There must be a less desperate way of earning a living." She preferred to play violin at weddings and bat and bar mitzvahs. Once, Sasha ran into her playing on the street, near Harvard Yard. She had a street performer permit, but could hardly compete with the more elaborate acts. Sasha didn't know what happened to her afterwards.

The office party gift that Sasha has unwrapped, from a secret giver, is a set of four microplane graters with color-coded handles. A smile works itself into the edges of her lips. The smile spreads wider and wider. She turned forty-two this year. Looking around the decorated conference room, she sees her coworkers immersed in the gift exchange. Soon, somebody will open the package she contributed: a notebook and a set of multicolored pens. The nonprofit they work for leads the fight against fossil fuels. Each person in the room is a dedicated environmentalist and each could launch, unprompted, into a rant against consumer culture and entrenched power structures.

One by one, the gifts are unwrapped, explained, cheered, appreciated. Theirs is a thankless job, and they've learned to put in time for teambuilding, to support one another.

The smile grows still wider on Sasha's face, as she pictures herself as that person with a microplane in each hand, one for the lemon, one for the lime. She can hear Jamie's voice. "Without professional tools a chef is just a housewife!" She stifles a laugh. On a different day, her coworkers would enjoy her story about Jamie, they really would.

A big feeling, like a bubble of warm air, grows in her chest. It's love and exhaustion, a sense of futility and a sense of being in the right place at the right time, the appreciation for how far they've come and how ludicrous their struggle seems compared to all the forces that are acting out in the world.

ACKNOWLEDGEMENTS

"Her Left Side," "Infestation," and "How to Deliver a Genius," first published in *World Literature Today* 91.1 (January 2017)

"A Wish," "Evasion," "Graduate School," "Her Turn," first published in the inaugural issue of *The Cove* (Spring 2018)

"Helen More's Suicide," first published in *Feminist Studies* 44.1 (Spring 2018)

"Dandelion," won second place in Eyelands Eighth International Short Story Contest, and appeared in an anthology *Luggage* (Fall 2018)

"My Mother at the Shooting Range," first published in *J Journal: New Writing on Justice* 3.1 (Spring 2010)

"Doctor Sveta," first published in *Alaska Quarterly Review 34, 3 &4* (Winter/Spring 2018)

"*Blan-Manzhe* with the Taste of Pears and Cream," first published in *Lunch Ticket* (Summer/Fall 2017)

"Cream and Sugar," first published in *the museum of americana* 15 (Summer 2018)

"Clock," first published in *Tin House's Open Bar* (January 2017)

"The Swallow," first published in *Narrative* magazine (June 2010)

"We Were Geniuses," first published in *The Provo Canyon Review* 1.1 (Spring 2013)

"Companionship," won Litquake's Fiction contest, was shortlisted for *Brilliant Flash Fiction's* "Wow Us" contest, and appeared in *Brilliant Flash Fiction* (September 2018)

"The Broken Violin," first published in *Prick of the Spindle* 1 (October 2011)

"Bananas for Sale," first published in *Scoundrel Time* (February 2019)
"Three Losses," first published in *DUM DUM Zine* 4 (February 2014)

There are a few reasons I started writing fiction in English. At the time, just after college, I had an audience of one: my husband David Grenetz. Back in college, in spare time between working three jobs and going to class, he proofread my marketing and economics essays, helping me earn steady As and fooling me into thinking I could master English. Later, when I turned to fiction, Dave kept asking me to write more time travel stories, but nevertheless he patiently read what I emailed him, fixed my grammar, and pointed out some of the ways my characters and scenes didn't make sense. Some years later, I noticed that I was relying less on his help with my grammar and more on his literary taste. I have so many things to thank Dave for; certainly, one of them is making the time to listen and read my stories, no matter how busy and tired he might be. Thank you.

I'm incredibly lucky to have a number of people in my life who have given my work thoughtful attention, who have encouraged my experiments, and inspired me by their own writing. My sincere gratitude to the early readers of this book: Karen E. Bender, Will Boast, Jennifer du-Bois, Anthony Marra, Peter Orner, and Hannah Pittard, and to generous friends and colleagues who have been with me through the writing and revision of these stories: Lauren Alwan, Olga Blomgren, Katie Bourzac, Leslie Kirk Campbell, Mari Coates, Caryn Cordello, Laurie Ann Doyle, Jacqueline Doyle, Lyndsey Ellis, Amber Hatfield, Marie Houzelle, Louis Gurman, Sarah Gurman, Scott Landers, Frances Lefkowitz, Cass Pursell, Bart Schneider, Anna Sears, Alicia Rouveral, Anna Sears, Alicia Rouveral, Alia Volz, Evelyn Walsh, Genanne Walsh, Elyse Weingarten, John Zic. I remember with gratitude Sunny V. Robinson, who shortly before she passed away read and commented on my first, raw, short fiction manuscript. Daria Moudroliubova showed me these could be a book. I'm honored and grateful to Olga Carlisle for her friendship and guidance.

ACKNOWLEDGEMENTS

Thank you to my teachers of Comparative Literature at San Francisco State University, Ellen Peel, Dane Johnson, and Shirin Khanmohamadi; to Tamim Ansary, Kurt Wallace Martin, Judy Viertel, James Warner, and the members of the San Francisco Writers Workshop who commented on my stories every Tuesday night; to Tom Jenks, Carol Edgarian, and Mimi Kusch, my mentors at *Narrative Magazine*. I'm incredibly grateful to Tom and Carol for the opportunity to work with the astonishing writers who appear in *Narrative*.

My deepest gratitude to Peg Alford Pursell who has been a true champion of so many writers and whose dedication to her writing practice has been an inspiration. It has been exhilarating to watch Peg gather a community of writers around Why There Are Words reading series and grow it into a national presence, and build WTAW Press from scratch. I'm delighted to be a part of this.

I dedicate this book to my family, which includes, in addition to Dave and our children, my parents Maria and Leonid Zilberburg, my brother Konstantin Zilberburg, and my aunt Maya Ovsyannikova. I grew up listening to stories told by captivating narrators. I don't take for granted my family's encouragement of me to tell these stories in my own way. Writing fiction requires a delicate balance of many elements, and if I manage to do so with any degree of complexity, it's thanks to them who constantly teach me that my perspective is but one among many.